THE]

Stacy Barnett Mozer

Spellbound River Press

THE PERFECT TRIP

Copyright © 2017 by Stacy Barnett Mozer
Cover and title page illustration by Lois Bradley
All rights reserved.

No part of this book may be used or reproduced by any means, graphic, electronic, or mechanical, including photocopying, taping, and recording without written permission except in the case of brief quotations embodied in critical articles and reviews.

This is a work of fiction. All the characters, organizations, and events portrayed in this novel are either products of the author's imagination or used fictitiously.

Spellbound River Press
PO Box 1084
Socorro, New Mexico 87801
www.spellboundriver.com

ISBN: 978-1-945017-23-0 (paperback)
ISBN: 978-1-945017-24-7 (digital edition)

Library of Congress Control Number: 2016956150

DEDICATION

For my parents, Jerry and Beth, and sister, Dana. Thank you for the joy and laughter of my childhood. I will always remember our perfect trip. I'm so fortunate to have you, then and now.

1

I pace back and forth as my stepmom, Nancy logs into her email account. "It's here!" she says. My four-year-old sister Deborah and I rush over and squeeze between Nancy and the wall to view the screen of her laptop. Nancy reaches down to click on the message, then stops and looks at me. "Shouldn't we wait for your dad?" she asks.

My eyes take in the unopened email, glance at Nancy, then go back to the email. Dad *will* be disappointed he's not here, but there's no way I can wait.

"*I'll* get Daddy," Deborah says. She picks up Nancy's phone from the table and in seconds my dad's face appears.

"Sammy's letter came," Deborah says to him.

"And?" he asks.

Nancy clicks on the email. We lean in closer. Deborah holds "Dad" up to the screen.

"What does it say?" Deborah asks. In all the excitement we almost forgot she doesn't know how to read. Reciting it aloud, I read, "Congratulations and welcome to the U14 Travel Team!"

"Yippee!" Deborah says. She jumps up and down and the ruffles on her purple tutu flutter with her excitement. A strand of her blonde hair falls loose around her face.

I continue, "Most of the team was together last year and now we've added five new players to the roster for the fall season. We definitely look forward to meeting each of our new teammates in person."

"Every person on this team is important, but we want to extend a special warm welcome to Samantha Barrette. Sam will be the first girl to play Travel Baseball since the town started this league. If you were at the U13 Championship game in June, you already know Sam comes to us based on her merit. I know you will join me in welcoming her and our other new players to the team. Practice starts the last week of August. I look forward to seeing you there."

Skimming through a part about equipment and August training, I almost can't believe it. It's too good to be true! After such a tough beginning to the summer—my former coach telling me I had an attitude and he wouldn't recommend me without a good camp report, and the baseball camp being upset I was a girl and putting me on the weaker team—things are finally hitting the sweet spot.

"The coach mentioned you personally," Nancy says, more to herself than to me. I read that part again. Deborah does a little spin and gives me a huge hug.

"Go Sammy!" she says.

"I'm so happy for you, Sam," Nancy adds. She gives me a big hug, too. A few weeks ago I wouldn't have believed my stepmom was happy about anything to do with me. How little I knew. Turns out she's one of my biggest fans.

"Way to go, Cracker Jack," Dad says. "We'll celebrate tonight when I get home. I have a meeting, but I shouldn't be too late." He pauses for a minute, then says, "Don't forget to call your mom, Sam. I'm sure she'll want to hear the great news."

Doubtful. This summer I realized Mom hasn't been interested in me for a very long time. On the phone she asks all the right supportive questions, but she didn't take me to baseball camp or pick me up as she promised, and she cancelled our summer trip. As far as I'm concerned, she can wait to hear the news, if ever. Besides, the first person I want to call is Mike.

Going back to my side of the table, I pick up my phone and dial him. Deborah looks over and smiles. "Sammy, are you calling your *boy*friend?"

"No," I say too quickly. She giggles. I slide out of my seat and walk into the hall before Mike hears her in the background. Ever since we came home from baseball camp, things have been different with us. We've always been good friends and teammates. But at baseball camp that changed into something more. Deborah caught him holding my hand when we were watching a movie on the couch. She finds the whole thing hilarious. I'm still not 100% sure what I think about it. It's cool and weird at the same time.

"Hey," I say, hoping I'm out of earshot. "I made it, can you believe it?"

"Yeah, I heard," Mike says. His voice sounds excited, but off.

"Well, we should go out. I mean, celebrate? You know, with pizza?" Shoot. Did I just ask him out on a real date?

"Not sure if I can but I'll text you," he says. "We're still packing."

"Sure, okay, that's fine," I say. Mike and his family are leaving in two days on a three-week camping trip. His parents have time for things like that because they're teachers. They're traveling from Connecticut to Wyoming and back, seeing all sorts of amazing things such as Mount Rushmore and the Rocky Mountains.

But a tingle in my stomach tells me packing's not why he doesn't want to see me. Before I can ask, he says, "Later, Sam," and hangs up the phone.

So weird. I would have thought he'd be excited I asked him to go out. Not knowing what to make of him, I need to talk to my best friend, Tasha. My finger reaches for her number, but she's only a few blocks away. Plus, we've barely seen each other this summer and she leaves next week for soccer camp.

"Nancy," I call, "I'm going over to Tasha's."

"Fine, Sam. Take your phone with you."

The pitter patter of little feet follows me down the hall. "Can I come, Sammy?" Deborah asks. "Please, can I?"

"Not this time, okay, Deb?"

She frowns, but doesn't argue. Instead she walks back to the kitchen, head down. I've been trying to spend more time with Deborah since I've been home from camp, but not this time. Not if we're going to be talking about Mike.

She'll get over it.

2

In the garage, I rummage through sports equipment until I find my bike and helmet. It's a warm day, but the wind is cooling. The town just repaved, so even though it's a busy road, I can stay to the side until I get to Tasha's turn off. I park my bike in her driveway and hurry up to her door. As if she can sense I'm here, she opens it as I'm about to knock.

"Hey," I say, taking a step backwards.

"So… did it come?" she asks without a hello.

Nodding, I show her the message Nancy forwarded me. She snatches my phone out of my hand and walks back into the house. I follow her inside and up two flights of stairs to her room. The staircase is so curvy I don't know how she reads and walks without tripping.

When we get to her room it looks like a clothes bomb went off. The only thing uncovered is her hammock chair, so I plop there on top of a couple of towels.

"Awesome. This is so great, Sam. Though…"

"Though, what?"

"Do you really think he needed to mention you? Specifically? It's kind of… I don't know?"

"Weird?" I add, which makes me think about Mike's tone.

"Kinda, yeah. What did Mike say?"

"He didn't really say much of anything," I humph. She raises her eyebrows.

"Yikes, not good. So he's mad."

I shrug. "I don't know why he should be, mad at me, I mean. It's not like I control what anyone else does."

"He's not mad, he's jealous. After all, he's new to the team too and it doesn't say people should remember his performance in that same game."

That's true, but still not my fault. Except that's last season's attitude talking in my head. At baseball camp I realized I'd been so busy thinking about the people rooting against me I didn't realize how my attitude was affecting my team. If our new coach had welcomed Mike to the team but not me, I would have been upset.

"So what do I do?" I ask Tasha. "Do I apologize?"

"What for? You didn't do anything wrong."

Groaning, I smack my hand against my head. This is so confusing.

"Look," Tasha says, "I say do nothing. By the time Mike gets back he'll only remember he *loves* you."

Well, that's good.

I guess.

It also makes me nauseous.

"Now can we talk about me?" Tasha asks. She pulls out her phone and shows me photos of her favorite soccer star, Mia Hamm. "Can you believe I'll be training with her next week? People might not know her now, but she led her soccer team to two Olympic gold medals and one silver. She's awesome!"

Tasha's so excited she's forgotten I know all about Mia from her third grade book report where we had to become someone famous and give a speech. A couple of kids told her she made a terrible Mia because Tasha's Jamaican and Mia's…not, but Tasha looked them in the face and said, "I can be anyone I want to be, just like Mia."

When I finally get home I expect Dad to come running but instead he's in the kitchen talking to Nancy in a hushed voice.

"Did someone die?" I ask, interrupting them.

"No, of course not," Dad says with a small clipped chuckle. "Why do you ask?"

I shrug. "The two of you seem so serious."

Dad smiles big. "Congratulations! Not that I'm surprised. What did Tasha and Mike say?"

It's strange Dad changed the subject, but if he says everything's fine, I believe him. Through the divorce and remarriage, he's always told me everything.

He leads me into the dining room even though we only use it for special occasions. I sit down at my usual place, next to Dad. Deborah is already there sitting across from us. Nancy has ordered sushi and Chinese food since she knows it's one of my favorites. It was either that or a juicy burger.

As Dad passes me a bowl of miso soup he says, "We're both so proud of you, Sam. You've worked so hard this summer. But we still have a bunch of weeks left and I think you'll enjoy what we're doing next."

"What, Daddy?" Deborah asks.

THE PERFECT TRIP

"You guys know how Mike and his family are going camping and how Sam keeps saying she wishes we could do a trip like that someday?"

"Yeah," I say, as I take some rice from the serving dish.

"Well, I spoke to Jim this afternoon and we're going with them!"

Rice spills all over the table as the serving fork slips out of my hand. "*Really?*" I say aloud. Next to baseball, camping was one of my favorite things to do with my parents. We'd never gone very far, but sleeping in a tent under the stars is like being in a different world. Even after the divorce, Dad and I still went camping on weekends. We stopped going when Dad married Nancy and Deborah was born. Dad even sold the equipment. But this trip is with Mike. Mike, who's mad at me.

Nancy gives me a look, almost like she knows what I'm thinking. I'll have to talk to her more about this later. Dad's still rattling off all the places we'll be visiting so I focus on that instead. By the end, I'm confused.

"How can we go to Wyoming? Won't it take too long?" Dad never takes off more than a week from work at a time.

"It *is* a long trip, it will take almost two weeks to get out there, but Jim and Amy have it all planned so it will be easy to tag along. And we're all staying with my parents in Wyoming."

"Nanny and Papa?" Deborah says. "We only see them when they come here in December!"

"Yep. They live right in Jackson Hole, and they're always begging us to visit. Sam, you went when you were a toddler, but I'm sure you don't remember."

A vague memory of trying to catch these little rodents that popped up out of the ground and were called whistle pigs flashes through my head. I still think of them every time I see a whack-a-mole game at an amusement park.

"Are we *all* going to go?" I ask. "Isn't camping too…messy?" I ask Nancy. I don't mean to be rude, but trying to picture her washing a pot outside or making a fire is impossible. She barely likes to rinse a dish before it goes into the dishwasher. I'll bet this is why they were talking quietly earlier. That's when Dad must have told her. Hopefully my question won't make her more upset.

Fortunately, she laughs.

"I will admit camping isn't really my thing. But I'm sure with you and your dad to help me, it'll be fun. And Jim and Amy go camping with Mike all the time so we won't have to figure everything out ourselves. They've been begging us to go with them for years. They're even lending us a tent and equipment."

Is Mike excited? I wonder. But I don't ask. Instead I say, "Deb, what do you think about going camping?" I can imagine my four-year-old, princess-dress-wearing sister on a camping trip as little as I can imagine Nancy.

She shrugs. "Is it fun, Sammy?"

"Camping is a ton of fun. You get to sleep in a tent and roast marshmallows and look at the stars."

"There's marshmallows? I love camping!" Deborah says.

"So when are we leaving?"

Nancy asks me to help her bring the dishes to the kitchen. It's a perfect time to talk to her about Mike, but before I can even put down one dish the doorbell rings. "I'll get it," I say.

Mike's standing on our stoop covered in camping equipment. My heart gives a little flip, or is it indigestion?

"My dad says you need camping supplies. I wasn't sure what, so I brought everything we aren't using. I think you should put the tent outside."

"Okay," I say. He's already walking through the house toward the yard.

Everything turns out to be an old yellow tent and a camping backpack full of smaller items. "The tent's kind of smelly so we should set it up. That way it can air out until we go this weekend," Mike says with absolutely no emotion.

He shows me what to do and, working in silence, we get it up quickly. The smell of stale air hits us as soon as I open the door. "When was the last time you took this tent camping?"

"Maybe last summer? Or the summer before. I'm not really sure. It's a good tent even though it's much harder to put up than the new ones. They practically put themselves up. That's what we have for our trip. I mean the trip *we'll both* be going on."

I know I didn't do anything wrong, but he's definitely upset about something. It was fine when I wasn't going to see him for a few weeks but now I'm going to see him every day.

As Mike opens all the windows of the tent I try to figure out what to say. But when he comes back outside he says, "You're all set," and turns to go.

"Mike," I call after him.

"Yeah, Sam?"

"I wanted to say sorry, about before. I should have realized you'd be upset Coach didn't mention you in the letter like he mentioned me."

Mike opens his mouth to say something but closes it again. "That's not it," he says.

"Then what?"

"I have to go," he says.

He walks out of my yard, leaving me alone with a musty tent.

The next day is a rush of planning and packing. Dad even stays home from work to help. Nancy sprays the whole tent with some sort of odor eater, and even though I think it's silly, it really makes a difference. I call Tasha and tell her we're spending our last night together in the tent.

As I'm heading out with my sleeping bag, Deborah comes running down the stairs in a pink puffy tutu. A princess sleeping bag trails behind her and a pink backpack is thrown over her shoulder. "Sammy, can I sleep in the tent with you and Tasha? Pleeze?"

I had hoped to use tonight to talk to Tasha about Mike, camping, and other *grown-up* stuff, but Deborah is so excited I can't let her down. "It's fine with me, as long as it's fine with Nancy. And you can't wear a tutu."

"Okay," she says a little reluctantly. She drops the stuff in a heap and pulls the tutu off her waist, revealing an actual pair of shorts. Leaving everything in the hallway, she bounces to the kitchen. I hear Nancy's footsteps a minute later.

"Are you sure you don't mind?" she asks.

I *do* mind, but not enough to say no. "It'll be fine. After all, she does have to get used to camping, doesn't she? And we'll be right outside in the yard."

"If you're okay, I'm okay," Nancy says. "But definitely get me if you have any problems."

What is Nancy so worried about? What problems could I have?

Tasha and I bring out a ton of junk food and nail polish. We spend the night eating, polishing, and joking around. Deborah even teaches us a new soccer card game Tasha loves. I don't think she has the rules right, but it's fun anyway. Finally, it's close to Deborah's bedtime and she yawns. I look at Tasha and she nods.

"Time for bed!" I say.

"Already?" Deborah asks.

"Yeah, it's *really* late," Tasha says, yawning loudly.

"Okay," Deborah says.

We head inside to brush our teeth and go to the bathroom, then come back out and get into our sleeping bags. With luck, Deborah will be out in minutes. "Good night," I say to them, lying down and pretending to close my eyes. Tasha's doing the same thing. My ears hear nothing but breathing. We may have done it!

Then, "Sammy, I can't sleep."

Oh well. I sit up and look at Tasha. "How 'bout we tell you a story?" I ask.

Deborah nods and claps her hands.

"What story should we tell?" Tasha asks. "A ghost story? I know a great one!"

I smack Tasha's arm. "Do you want her to be up all night?"

"Oh, right," she whispers back. Tasha only has two brothers. She doesn't always know what to do with little sisters.

Deborah reaches into her bag and takes out a couple of small rubber princesses. "I want a princess story," she says. She opens the bag again and takes out a large plastic horse. "With horses." I'm always amazed at how much she fits in this little bag. It's like she's a miniature Mary Poppins.

Tasha looks at me and shrugs. What story should I tell? When Deborah was little I used to tell her Deb and Sammy stories to get her to sleep. I'll just make this one larger. I begin, "Once upon a time there was a princess named Deborah who took a royal journey across America."

"Yeah," Tasha continues, taking my lead. "She traveled in her royal horse and buggy."

"Horse and buggy? Princesses ride in carriages, Tasha," Deborah cuts in.

I laugh.

"*What?* She wanted a horse," Tasha says out of the side of her mouth.

Shaking my head, I continue, "Princess Deborah traveled in her *royal carriage* with the king and queen and her older sister, Princess Sammy."

"Samantha," Deborah breaks in. "Princesses have big names."

"Fine, Samantha. But the family didn't know Princess Deborah had a special power—she could speak to horses."

"Nice," Tasha whispers.

For the next, what seems like forever but is probably about a half an hour, I continue the story with Tasha jumping in every now and again to add a not-quite-helpful detail. Princess Deborah and her best friend, a grey horse named Misty, visit all the places we'll be going on our trip. Tasha stops me to ask about some of them. As I am telling Tasha about Wyoming, Tasha puts her finger to her lips.

"Shhh. I think she's finally asleep." She points to Deborah.

The two of us lean in closer and watch Deborah breathe. Her chest moves up and down and her eyes are closed. She's asleep.

Yawning myself, I motion for Tasha to come outside so we won't accidentally wake Deborah up.

It's a beautiful night. Warm, but not too hot. Nancy insisted on leaving a light on the deck so it's bright in front of the tent. Using our phones as flashlights, I lead Tasha to the hammock, which is closer to the woods, beyond the light.

"So, are you finally going to tell me about Mike?" Tasha asks once we are lying down.

"I don't know what there is to tell. I tried to talk to him. But he said he wasn't mad about Coach's note and that it's something else. What else could it be?"

"Just because he *says* that's not it, doesn't mean that's not what it is."

"I guess."

We lie there for a while, thinking. The hammock sways side to side, moving in time to our breathing. A light breeze blows across my nose. I can just make out the stars through the trees. I close my eyes and listen to the bullfrogs in the pond next door…

A loud sound jars me awake and I bolt upright. Tasha moves too and in seconds we're flipping and twirling and landing on the ground.

"Ouch," Tasha says.

"Did you hear something?" I ask.

We listen. At first the only sounds are the frogs. Then, "Sammy!!! Sammy!!! MOMMY!!!"

Deborah. Jumping up, I head for the tent. It's not day, but it's light enough to see. Rays of sun peek through the trees and there's a light mist on the ground. Tasha and I must have slept for a while.

The tent door opens, revealing Deborah huddled in a corner with her sleeping bag pulled around her like a shield. Tears line her face and her cheeks are red. She turns to me but her eyes are angry, not grateful. "There was a spider and you, you left me," she says. "You and Tasha. You left me alone. In a tent. Outside. With a spider," she adds again.

"I'm sorry, Deb, we didn't mean to. Really." I try to put my arms around her but she pulls away. The tent door opens and I expect to see Tasha, but instead Nancy rushes in. She cuddles Deborah in her arms.

"Mommy, Sammy left me," Deborah says.

Nancy shoots me *the look*, and turns to Deborah. "It's okay, sweetie. I'm here now. I'm sure your sister has a great explanation, right, Samantha?"

She must really be mad if she's calling me Samantha again. "We didn't want to wake her so we went out to the hammock to talk. We fell asleep. It was an accident."

Nancy sighs. "We'll discuss it later," she says. "Come on, Deborah. Let's go inside and wash your face."

Once they leave, Tasha comes in and sits next to me on the floor. "We really messed this one up, huh?"

It was definitely a foul ball.

Tasha gathers her stuff and heads home. I head upstairs to my room. Dad and Nancy are talking softly behind their door. I debate going down the hall to listen and see how much trouble I'm in, but if I get caught things will be worse. Plus, Dad and Nancy aren't my real problem. I knock on Deborah's door instead.

"If you're Sammy, go away," she calls.

"Please, Deb, the Horse Princess would forgive her sister. You know I didn't mean to leave you."

She doesn't answer.

I stand there for a couple more minutes just in case she changes her mind.

She doesn't.

Sighing, I go to my room to finish packing. The hiking backpack Mike brought over has a million pockets. Inside the bag I've stashed everything I think I will need: a Frisbee which folds up into a small pouch, trail mix for the road or hike munching, a metal water bottle with a built in straw, a tiny pocketknife that doesn't actually have any knives but came with a pretty good pair of scissors, music to listen to in the car, a back up solar charger, a small flashlight, and a tablet with a bunch of downloaded books.

I also pack a baseball bat, a couple of balls, and my glove. I don't know where I'll play, but a baseball player is always prepared.

Someone knocks on my door. "Come in," I say. Dad opens the door. He's dressed in cargo shorts, an orange shirt, and a vest that has lots of pockets. It's an outfit he hasn't worn in a long time. He comes in and sits down on my bed.

"Sam, I realize you didn't mean to leave your sister by herself, but it wasn't good. She almost refused to go on the trip."

"I'm sorry, Dad. I really am. Sometimes it's hard that she's so much younger. I want to include her, I really do."

"Nine years is a lot. But we have a lot of changes coming soon and she'll need her big sister to look out for her. Okay?"

I nod. It really will be hard for Deborah to be in the great outdoors when she can't handle a spider in our backyard.

"Dad?" I want to tell him about Mike but don't know what to say. I don't think Dad's given much thought to the two of us somewhat dating. We've known Mike and his family for so long, and it won't be the first time we've taken a trip together.

"What is it, Cracker Jack?"

"Does Mom know we're going on this trip? Does she know I made the Travel Team?"

Dad sits next to me. "Your mother always knows about everything happening in your life. She just isn't good at the being here part."

"I wish she were good at both."

"I know. But you have to believe she thinks she's doing what's best for you, even if it doesn't feel like it."

I doubt that. She always does what's best for her. I hug my dad's arm and lean into his shoulder. I can always count on him—and Nancy.

"Okay," he says. "There's just one more thing." Dad points around the room. "We're going to get this place cleaned while we're away. Can you make sure everything is where it should go instead of all over the floor?"

Surveying the mess, I think, *It's not that bad.* Most of the items on the floor are things I thought I'd take with me, but decided against. When Dad leaves I open my double door closet and place everything into the three-drawer rolling shelf. I make my bed, smoothing my green and white comforter and placing a matching pillow on top. After straightening the trophies on my desk and centering the signed baseball bat on the wall, I look around again. A cleaning service should have no trouble vacuuming and dusting.

I carry my bags downstairs and go to the kitchen for lunch. Deborah is already eating a peanut butter and jelly sandwich. She doesn't look at me as I come in. She really knows how to put a knife in my heart. After I eat my sandwich, I help Dad finish packing the car. Nancy's suitcase is huge!

"Are you planning to move there?" I ask her jokingly as she comes out to put a few cooking items into the car.

She doesn't laugh. "Well actually, Sam…"

Deborah pushes by us and gets into the car, interrupting whatever Nancy was going to say. Nancy buckles her into her booster seat.

I slide into the car through the other side and wince looking at Deborah's backpack. Unlike mine, which is made for camping, she used the same pink plastic one from yesterday, the one with a large picture of a princess on the front. Her outfit matches the pack. She's wearing a sparkly pink shirt that says, "Little Princess." Her hair is piled in a mess of curls surrounded by an even sparklier pink crown. Add a pair of long white gloves and the outfit would have been complete. At least she's still wearing shorts instead of a tutu.

"What's all that?" I ask, pointing to her bulging bag.

"I need stuff," she says coldly. She reaches into her bag and pulls out a little plastic Cinderella doll and a bunch of dresses.

"Oh no, we did that last time, remember? On the way to baseball camp. Cinderella's married and is living happily ever after with her prince. She doesn't need any dress changes."

"If she does, I'll do it myself." She crosses her arms in a humph. I've never seen her this mad. She's usually a big-hug-and-forget-about-it type of kid.

A knock on my window switches my attention away from Deborah. Tasha is propped on her bike in the street next to the car. I can't roll the window down because the car's not on, so I jump out and we move to the curb. I make sure to open Deborah's door too, but she stays in the car.

"Hey, I thought you went home."

"I just came to gloat. While you'll be covered with bugs and dirt, I'll be meeting my new best friend, Mia Hamm."

"Hey!"

"Don't worry, you'll still be in my top two." Tasha looks over at Deborah, who's still pouting. "Well, I'm out. Good luck, Sam."

"I think I'm going to need it."

She gives me a giant hug and bikes away. Dad gets in and starts up the car.

"Mommy, can you put on my CD?" Deborah asks as soon as Nancy sits down. Nancy turns in her seat and smiles. It's weak, but it's still a smile. I grin back at her, hoping my enthusiasm for this adventure will brighten her mood.

"Deborah, I think we listened to your princess music enough last time. Why don't we let your sister pick a station to start the trip?"

Deborah turns to me expectantly. "Princess music," she demands.

How can I argue? Nancy doesn't even wait for me to respond before a screechy princess starts singing Deborah's name as we pull away from the curb.

This first part of the trip is familiar. Mike's parents decided we should stay in New Jersey tonight so Nancy and Deborah can get used to being in a tent while we're still close to home. I can see the back of Mike's head through the window of his car. He hasn't responded to my "hi" text.

We cross the George Washington Bridge. I'm looking out the window at the water when I hear, "Sammy."

"Yeah?" I say.

"Do you think Princess Deborah would stay mad at her sister if she left her in the woods with a spider?" Deborah says.

She's forgiven me. "I think Princess Deborah would understand the only reason Princess Samantha would leave her is if she didn't have a choice," I think for a minute, "For instance, if she fell under a sleeping spell."

She nods. "Maybe you could tell me that story?"

"Sure."

Off and on, for the next two hours, I continue the story of Princess Deborah. After Princess Samantha is placed under a sleeping spell, a giant spider comes to steal Princess Deborah. Fortunately, Princess Deborah's horse Misty saves the day and whisks Princess Deborah away from the spider. The two of them find Princess Samantha and save her too.

Nancy turns around and smiles at me as I tell the story and I can tell I've been forgiven. If only making up with Mike were this easy.

"Hey look, isn't that it?" Nancy asks as the cars approach a big sign with a tent next to a gravel road.

"But the story's not over," Deborah whines.

"So Princess Deborah and Misty gallop into the sunset after forgiving her sister," I tell her.

"The end," she adds.

We follow Mike's car onto a small dirt road. A second sign with words made out of logs reads, "Pine Tree Camp Grounds." The path fits the name. Giant pines surround us on all sides. Occasionally a tent can be seen among the trees. At one site a dozen or so people are standing around together.

Nancy rolls down her window and takes in a deep breath. "Smells...piney," she says. She sneezes. I try not to laugh. This really is going to be tough for her.

Deborah rolls down her window too and wrinkles up her nose. "It's weird," she says. "What is it?"

"Campfires and pine trees," I say.

"And marshmallows?" Deborah asks.

"Not until later," I tell her.

"Is it later yet?" she asks.

We pull up in front of a small building, the only real building in sight. Mike's dad gets out of the car. "I'll go in with Jim and check in," Dad says.

My impatience gets the better of me. "Can I get out and look around?" I ask Nancy.

"That's fine. As long as you don't go too far and you bring Deborah with you."

Deborah's face lights up and she leaps out of the car, pausing only to grab a pair of fairy wings out of her bag. "Come on, Sammy, let's go," she says, grabbing my hand.

"Nancy," I say, looking for some help.

"What?" she asks. I point to the wings.

"Well, it could be worse, Sam," she says.

"How?"

Nancy whispers in my ear, "She could have asked you to wear them."

Good point. My hand grasps Deborah's and I pull her down the road before she gets any ideas. Nancy walks over to talk to Mike's mom, Amy. Mike is standing next to his car. "Mike, Mike," Deborah says as we pass him, "Can you come with us? We're taking a walk. In the woods!"

Mike looks at me and looks like he's about to say no, but Deborah doesn't give him a choice. She grabs his hand and forces him to walk with us.

The path winds through the woods past a few more campsites. We can hear the sounds of people all around us, mostly because no one is talking.

"Just think, Deb," I say to break the silence, "tonight we are going to be sleeping in a tent in the real woods!"

"Will you leave me again, Sammy?" she asks. Her voice trembles a bit.

"She left you?" Mike asks, raising his eyebrows.

"Tasha and I fell asleep on the hammock. We didn't mean to leave her alone."

Mike rolls his eyes and looks away. Seriously, what did I do?

"Hey," I tell Deborah, "there's absolutely nothing to worry about. Besides, Nancy and Dad will be sleeping in the tent with you, too."

"But what about bears?" she asks.

"Bears? I don't think there are any bears," Mike says.

"You don't *think* there are bears? So there might be bears?" Deborah says. I shoot Mike a *not helping* look, but he's already looked away.

Sounds of cooing and giggling come from one of the campsites nearby. A woman is sitting in a pop-up chair playing with a baby. It gives me an idea.

"Deb, look over there. See that baby?" I ask.

"Yeah?"

"Do you think that woman would bring a *baby* into the woods if she was worried about bears?" I made sure to stress the word baby. Deborah's as into babies as she is into princesses. Her eyes brighten and I know I've found the right tactic.

"No, Sammy, you're right. No one would bring a *baby* into a wood full of bears."

"Besides," I add to be safe, "you're a princess. Princesses love the woods. It's where they make their homes. If we're lucky, we might even catch a glimpse of Misty. She's always close by, you know."

Deborah grins. She squeezes our hands and we continue to walk through the woods. She keeps peering at each campsite, probably looking for babies and a grey horse.

"Ouch," she says suddenly.

"What's wrong?" I ask.

"I have a bug bite. Look!" She holds up her arm for me to see. As I examine her bite, I feel a few pinches on the back of my legs.

Now that she's mentioned it, my legs itch too. I reach down and realize I've gained a number of bites below the end of my shorts. I feel one, two, six separate bites.

"Let's go back to the car and get some bug spray," I tell them.

"You didn't put any on before walking?" Mike says.

"No."

"Well, that wasn't too bright. Come on." He turns and runs back to the car.

We follow. Jim and Dad are chatting with Amy and Nancy. "Are you ready?" Dad says.

"Not quite." I direct Deborah to the back of the car and pull out the bug spray. Filling the air with mist, I'm careful not to get it into our faces. Hopefully that will get the bugs to stand down.

We get back into our cars and drive to the campsite. It's a decent spot, not too close to other people but not in the middle of the woods either, in eyesight of a bathroom. While Mike and his dad pop up their tent, Dad pulls out the directions for the one we've borrowed. He opens them up and looks them up and down. He turns the page sideways and backwards.

"What's wrong?" I ask.

"I think tents must have been put up differently the last time I put one up."

"I'm pretty sure this tent is as old as the ones you are used to," I say. "But let me show you."

"Sure, Cracker Jack, tell me what to do."

I smile and we get to work.

We're just about done when Mike comes over. He and his parents have already taken out all their supplies and organized the food. "Do you need help?" he asks.

"So now you're talking to me?"

"My mom told me to ask you." I look over and she waves.

I wave back. "I'm fine, thank you very much," I say to Mike though clenched teeth. He hesitates for a moment, then goes back to his mom. She shakes her head and musses his hair.

I knock in the next spoke and it's all done.

"Good job," Jim calls to us. He gives me two thumbs up.

We check to make sure the tent is solid, then go inside to spread out our sleeping bags. I place mine all the way on the side, next to a window. Nancy stands in the middle of the tent looking all around.

"What's wrong?" I ask her.

"Is there a plug someplace?"

"In a tent?"

She gives a small sigh. "The guy at the camping store said people bring air mattresses to sleep on so I bought one. I should have thought about the fact that there wouldn't be electricity."

My lips clench trying to hold back the laughter but my shoulders are probably giving me away. "There usually is one at the campsite someplace. It's probably by where we parked the car. And don't those things come with a car plug?" I ask.

She looks at the box. "Oh, yeah, it does! What would I do without you?" She kisses the top of my head. It's odd, but nice. Motherly. "Do you want to come outside and help me with it?" she asks.

Her eyes look toward the door and back at Dad, and it makes me think she's trying to talk to me privately again. I need to talk to her too. I might know more about camping than Nancy, but I'd put money on her knowing more than me about what's going on with Mike.

I change positions to join her and the stinging from my legs comes back in full force. I need to scratch but if Nancy notices my legs she'll freak out. Worse, she'll turn us around and have us head back home.

"I'm going to stay and set things up in here," I say.

She nods, but her face looks a little crestfallen. She asks my dad to help her instead.

As soon as she leaves, I pull on sweat pants. I organize my things while Dad and Nancy go to blow up the mattress. They come back and have to hold it sideways to get it through the door. It's big, bigger than what people usually bring camping. More like something you'd use for an extra bed in a house. It takes up half the tent.

Deborah runs into the tent and her eyes light up. "Oh, yay! A bouncy thing!" she says. She springs off the ground. Nancy catches her mid-air. "Oh no, you don't. We have to sleep on this for a long time. Lying down only, without shoes." Giving me a nod that reads, *Keep an eye on her*, she and Dad go outside to help Mike's parents with dinner.

"Only lying down," Deborah repeats when they are gone. She drags her sleeping bag onto the middle of the air mattress and lies down on top of it. I'll let them deal with that later.

Reaching into my bag, I pull out my phone to text Tasha. No service. Not even a bar. No Wi-Fi either. Holding the phone up, I take some pictures of the tent so I can send them to her later, making sure to capture Deborah taking up most of the mattress. As I change directions, my legs prickle and burn. I pull up my pants legs and notice they've grown in size. They're also a little warm to the touch. Trying not to think about the heat, I pull my pants legs back down and go back to ignoring them.

A mouth-watering smell tells me dinner will be ready soon. Mike's family had us pitch in for a large cooler of meat and I can practically taste the hamburgers.

"Come on, squirt," I say to Deborah. "It smells like dinner time. Let's get out there."

"Do you think there'll be French fries?" she asks.

"No fries," I say. "No ovens."

"Oh," she says, a bit disappointed.

Her eyes light up though when she sees Amy cooking corn over the fire. There are also full-fat potato chips, a treat we don't get a lot at home. Deborah grabs some quick before Nancy can say no.

As I sit down my pants rub against my bug bites, irritating them more. I scratch through the pants, but it just makes them worse. Biting into my hamburger while listening to the adults talk, I try not to think about them, or about Mike sitting as far away from me as possible.

"So," Dad says to Nancy and Deborah after we've cleared our plates. "This isn't too bad, is it?"

"I'm having fun, Daddy," Deborah says.

"And now we have another surprise," Amy says. She holds out a package of marshmallows and a bunch of chocolate bars.

"S'MORES!" Deborah yells.

"Yep! After we eat we need the three of you to find some branches we can use. Okay?" Jim says, looking at Mike and me.

"Sure," I say. Who doesn't love s'mores? I stand up and the burning sensation I'd experienced in the tent turns into light pain. Dad gives me a look. I resist the urge to scratch.

"Will they be okay in the woods?" Nancy asks Amy.

"They'll be fine. Don't worry. Mike and Sam can take care of Deborah," Amy says.

Nancy doesn't look convinced. She looks at me and nods towards Deborah. I nod back. Of course I'll take care of her.

"Come on, Deb," I say. "Let's find some good sticks."

The shadows are a bit longer but we can still see. I keep Deborah by my side. Mike forges ahead, barely waiting for us. Not far from the campsite, we find some long, dry branches that have good spots for holding marshmallows. I hand one to Deborah and we turn to head back. She goes first. When she's far enough away, I pull Mike aside.

"Are you going to act this way the whole trip? I thought you liked me."

"I did, I mean I do, I mean I don't know, Sam. You can be so self-centered sometimes. At camp I got why. That kid Chris was bullying you. I saw that. But I just wish you'd..."

"I'd what?"

He shrugs. "Worry about me sometimes, I guess. I don't know."

He turns away and walks back to the campsite. I follow, then realize I can't see Deborah anywhere. Have I really left her again? Nancy will kill me! I don't want to call for her because that will get everyone worried, so instead I brush past Mike and do my best baseball sprint around the bases.

Branches scratch my face as I break through the woods and reach the campsite. I scan the area and breathe out a sigh of relief. Deborah is by the fire with Nancy trying to put a marshmallow on her stick. Thank goodness. Nancy looks over at me with a question in her eye. I hope she can't see on my face that I almost abandoned Deborah again.

No matter what I do, I keep striking out.

I stand at the plate and stare down the pitcher. He looks familiar, but I can't figure out where I've seen him before. "You think you're so great, hit this," he yells at me.

"Bring it," I say. But my legs feel like jelly. I can't get into a good position.

The pitcher holds the ball in front of him and breathes out. I blink as a stream of fire leaves his lips and clings to the ball. Unconcerned about the heat, the pitcher goes into his wind up and releases. I want to duck out of the way, but know I must be seeing things, so I hold firm and use the bat as my weapon. It's a direct hit. The ball should be soaring away from me, but instead the flames consume the bat. I try to scream but no words form. The heat rushes over me, moving down my body and targeting my legs. They get hotter and hotter...

"Sam, wake up," Nancy's voice says. She lightly shakes my arm.

"Is Sammy okay?" Deborah calls from the air mattress. She ended up sleeping with Nancy, forcing my dad to the floor.

The burning sensation from my dream hasn't gone away now that my eyes are open. My legs have doubled in size and they do feel like they're on fire. "I think there's something wrong with my legs," I tell Nancy. My teeth find my lip and I bite down to hold back the tears. Nancy pulls up my pants and looks at some of the bites.

"Jeff, get up," she calls to my dad.

"I thought we were on vacation," my dad yawns.

"Jeff, you need to get up. It's Sam."

Dad comes over and tries to lift my pants legs. They won't go over the bites. He looks at his watch. "The front office opens at 7:00. I'll tell Jim, then go over there to find out if there are any doctors nearby."

Dad pulls on his clothes and leaves the tent. Deborah comes over and snuggles next to me, leaning a little on my legs. I gently move her to the side, not wanting any pressure on them.

"What's wrong, Sammy?" she asks.

"Your sister's legs are a bit swollen," Nancy says, answering for me. "Daddy is going to see if we can get some help."

Deborah jumps up and races across the tent to her backpack. She pulls out a magic wand and comes back over to where I'm sitting. She waves the wand over me and says some words I don't understand. She gives me a kiss. "All betta?" she asks.

"Much," I say through closed teeth. I try not to wince.

Dad comes back and tells Nancy the nearest hospital is twenty miles away.

"I think we should take down the tent before we go," Dad says. "We can continue the trip from there."

"Let's talk outside," Nancy says, which is code for an adult discussion.

Forcing myself to get up, I hobble to the bathroom. It's not far, but every step burns. Suddenly Mike's at my side. I'm so surprised I don't know what to say. "Here," he says, "my parents told me about your legs. Lean on me." He places his arm under my shoulders to help me walk. Why's he being so nice? Mike brings me to the door and starts to step inside.

"Girls room," I say, pointing to the sign.

"Oh, right. I'll be here, okay."

I nod. Sitting down to use the toilet brings on additional pain. I've had swelling from bug bites before, but this is ridiculous. Maybe it's some kind of Zika virus. My eyes water. I brush away the tears.

When Mike and I get back, Dad and Nancy still haven't come to a decision. Amy says, "You guys go take care of Sam. We'll take down the tent and meet you at the hospital."

"Thanks," Dad says to her. Nancy gives her arm a squeeze and helps me into the car. The twenty-minute ride feels like forever. Deborah tries to cheer me up by making faces and singing, but I barely pay attention. I limp into the emergency room and sit down. Dad keeps tapping his foot and pacing as the time drags on.

"What's taking them so long?" he asks Nancy.

"I don't know, honey."

"At this rate we're never going to get to the next campsite."

"Jeff," Nancy scolds.

"What? They're just bug bites."

Nancy looks like she wants to smack him. I feel terrible, and not because of the bites.

"Dad," I say, "I'm really sorry. I don't want to ruin everything."

Dad's eyes turn to me and it's like he's just remembered I'm here, but he gives me a bright smile. "No worries, Sam. They'll fix you up."

Nancy doesn't say anything but she bites her lip and looks away. I can almost see the route home plotting out in her head. We don't say much else for a while.

Finally, the doctor calls me in. Dad and Nancy come with me. Deborah stays outside with Mike and his family, who've had enough time to take down the tents and join us. The doctor looks at the bites, takes my temperature, checks my breathing, and has his nurse spread a strong smelling medicine on my legs.

"The good news is that the swelling is local. She doesn't appear to have any further reaction. I suggest soaking in a nice cool bath and massaging her legs with rubbing alcohol to take away the sting and burning. I'll also give you some Benadryl. It's an over the counter medicine, should this happen again."

He talks to my dad as if I'm not in the room. I hate when doctors do that. They're *my* legs, after all.

"Doctor, we're on a camping trip," my dad says.

"Well, I would suggest staying in a hotel tonight. She really needs to soak her legs and get away from the bugs."

"We understand," Nancy growls. She gives Dad a look that tells him not to stop arguing. He lowers his head and agrees.

A pit forms in the bottom of my stomach. I was supposed to be the one to encourage Nancy and Deborah on this trip, not convince them that camping is terrible. "We're going home, aren't we?" I say to them.

"What? Oh no. We can't... I mean, we have the whole trip planned," Dad says. He looks at Nancy.

She sighs. "We'll find a place to stay that's on our way so we can skip one night of camping and meet Jim and Amy at the next site."

"So we aren't going home?" I ask.

"No," Nancy says. There's a tone in her voice. One that says that this conversation isn't over.

We say goodbye to Mike's family and head to the motel. The doctor gave me some pain killers, so I sleep in the car and wake up when we get there. The place is pretty typical, two beds with green leaf comforters and a tiny bathroom.

At least it has a clean tub. Nancy prepares the bath with some sort of powder the doctor gave us. I submerge my legs until they stop burning. It feels like heaven, even if the place is a little dingy and smells slightly more mildewy than the tent. Nancy whips out the fabric spray.

Later that night, after the swelling has gone down, I lie in bed next to Deborah, who is sound asleep. Nancy and Dad are sitting outside talking quietly. I take out my phone to text Tasha. I have a ton of messages from her to read first.

"WHAT IS THIS?"

She's attached a photo of my house. In front of it is a sign. I zoom in closer. It says, "For Sale." What on Earth?

Tasha has a series of OMG texts after that, all panicked, asking me to get in touch. She says she was driving past my house and saw the sign. This has to be a mistake. I get out of bed to go ask Dad about it but their voices at the window stop me. I crouch down and listen.

"What are we going to do?" Nancy whispers.

"You heard the doctor, Sam's going to be fine," Dad says. "He said it's unlikely she'll react like this again, and if she does, we can use the Benadryl."

"That's not what I mean, and you know it," Nancy says. Her tone is sharp. I hold my breath. Whatever she is upset about, it must be serious.

"We can afford to pay for a couple nights of hotels," Dad says.

"But the house," Nancy says. I lean closer to the window. Here it is.

"I'll call Ted and fix the mistake with the house. Everything will be fine," Dad says.

I fall backwards on the floor and lie on the ground. I'm so relieved. I knew it had to be a mistake. I text Tasha, "Big mistake. All good."

"Thank heaven on earth," she texts back. "Town not same w/o U."

"Ask Mia to move in."

"Wouldn't be U."

"☺"

"So, Mike?"

THE PERFECT TRIP

I want to tell her about Mike, but not now. I text that I'm too tired and get back into bed. I close my eyes, thankful that at least this is going to be fine.

8

"What are we doing about tonight?" Nancy asks Dad at breakfast. We're at a small diner next to the motel. It smells like grease and bacon.

"What do you mean, what are we going to do?" Dad asks. "We have a reservation at a campsite in Ohio."

"Is that wise?" Nancy says, looking at me. "Maybe we need to stay inside another night."

"I'm sure Sam would prefer to go back to camping," Dad says.

"Yes, Nancy, I really would," I agree. "And we have the medicine now just in case."

"And I know Deborah wants to go too, right Deb?" Dad says. "Tonight we will be at the waterpark campsite in Ohio."

Deborah's eyes light up. She wasn't totally excited about the whole trip, but there are things she can't wait to see. On the list are snow-topped mountains, a rowboat, and this campground that has a waterpark.

"The one with the slides?" she squeals. "I can go on them, right, even if they are sooo big?"

"Yep," Dad says. "Even the ones that are sooo big."

"Please, please, please, please, can we go there tonight? Come on, Mommy, we have to go!" The seat bounces under her.

"Fine," Nancy says. She's trying not to smile, but it's impossible to say no to Deborah. "I will have to look around and check out the mosquito situation. And you, Sam, are going to have to wear pants even if it is hot."

"Fine, Nancy," I say. I will wear a full suit of armor if it means continuing this trip outside.

"Okay, it is settled," Dad says gleefully.

We finish our meal and head to the car. Deborah continues to bounce up and down in her seat. She's making me dizzy. Finally, I ask, "How about a Princess Deborah story?"

"Okay, but Princess Samantha isn't allowed to have anything happen to her legs."

I shut my mouth because that was the story I planned to tell. Except Princess Samantha's legs were going to swell up due to another spell. "Why not?"

She doesn't answer.

"Deb?"

"I don't want to think about that, okay?"

Wow, my trip to the hospital must have really bothered her. "Okay. No legs." I think quickly. "How 'bout I tell you about the time Princess Deborah stopped a galloping herd of horses just by putting up her hand?"

"Yes, that one!"

The story continues through Pennsylvania. Deborah takes a nap just as we get to the Ohio border, allowing me to relax until we get to the campground.

The moment we pull in I know I'm going to hate this place. The first thing we pass is a giant swimming pool with water slides. The mini-golf course across from it has the only waterfall we'll probably see. Short trees are speckled through the area amongst lots and lots of RVs. I stick out my tongue.

Deborah, on the other hand, is bouncing on her seat again. "Look, Sammy, an ice cream store. And a playground. Can we go to the playground? Pleeze??"

"Real showers!" Nancy says under her breath as we pass the bathhouse.

I shake my head.

"What?" she says. "I camped."

"For one night."

"It was a long night."

We both giggle. It's nice to joke with her. I feel like I cheated myself out of getting to know her all this time because I was angry she married my dad. Pretty stupid.

"Mommy, can we go play?" Deborah asks as soon as Dad stops the car at the office.

"As long as you both spray yourself head to toe with bug spray and as long as Sam and Mike stay with you."

"How can there be mosquitoes? There's no grass." I say.

"Sam," Dad warns.

I click my tongue. We should explore the place, not hang out on the playground. Nancy hears the click and stares me down.

"Fine," I say reluctantly.

"Yippee!" Deborah sings. Mike's already here, waiting. Deborah grabs him and the three of us walk over to the playground. He has definitely let go and moved on from what was bothering him. Instead of avoiding me, he's giving kind glances and the start of a smile. "Push me, push me!" Deborah says. She gets on a very ancient-looking turning thing.

"I can push both of you. If you want," Mike says.

I shake my head. The car ride and this place already have me a little nauseous. "Thanks, though. I can help you push."

He nods and we both take a side. "Hold on tight," I say to Deborah, then we both start running. After a couple of turns it's going faster than we are so we have the choice to either let go or jump on. I jump on. Mike does too.

"Wheee!" Deborah says.

"Wheee!" Mike and I say together.

The thing spins and spins. I see the office, the pool, the mini-golf, the RVs, the office, the pool, the mini-golf, the RVs. My stomach gives a lurch and I think I'm going to be sick. I try to stand up and get off.

"Hang on, there," Mike says. He holds my arm tight, and slowly drags a foot on the ground to slow us down. Once we've stopped, he helps me off. "You okay?" he asks.

I nod, wobbly.

"And your legs? Are they better now?"

I nod again.

"I'm glad. When my parents said you needed to go to the hospital I was…worried. I wouldn't want anything bad to happen, to you, I mean."

"Thanks," I say, finally finding my voice. I think my stomach is settling.

"The slide next," Deborah says, pointing to a twisty slide attached to a clubhouse that makes up the only other outdoor part of this playground. The rest is a glass enclosed indoor part, which reminds me of the kind of playground found at McDonalds. That's what this place is, the fast food of campgrounds.

"I think I need to sit for a minute, but you guys go," I say.

"You want me to sit with you?"

I do. Now that he is talking to me I might finally find out why he's been acting weird, but Deborah is waiting.

"That's okay. I'll watch and join you guys soon."

He nods and says to Deborah, "Race you to the top!"

Mike pretends to run really fast, while letting her catch up and get ahead of him. They go up and down, laughing together. It's actually nice to not have to be the only one entertaining her for once, and even nicer that Mike doesn't seem to mind playing with Deborah, and spending time with me.

9

Our parents call us over to the car and we drive to our "campsite," even though it's close enough to walk. The site is an open space in back of a bunch of RVs near some trees and a small brook. I try to convince everyone to place the tents facing backwards so at least it seems like we are in the trees, but everyone laughs as if I'm joking. Only Amy seems to get it. "It's only for one night," she says. "Why don't we have the tents face each other?"

Everyone agrees.

Once the tents are up, we go inside to change into bathing suits. I wish we were going to a lake instead of a water park, but the slides do look fun.

"Oh, no," Nancy says before I can start to change my clothes. "You're staying in long pants until we are absolutely sure you are not going to react to the bugs."

"Dad," I beg, looking to him.

Dad shrugs his shoulders. "Nothing I can do here, Cracker Jack. But don't worry. I'm sure there will be other places to swim this trip. And it's not like it's a lake."

He knows me well.

We leave the tent and find Mike's family ready with their towels. Mike looks me up and down and takes in the jeans. "You're not going?" he asks.

"Not allowed," I say, pointing to my legs.

He stands there for a moment, looking at me, at the pool, and at me again. "Hey, Dad," he calls to Jim. "If Sam can't go swimming, do the two of us have to go to the pool at all? Can we hang out around here or go walk around?"

Jim looks at Amy. "It's fine with me," she says.

"Just make sure to be back by 6:00 for dinner," Nancy says.

"You're not coming?" Deborah says to Mike.

"Not this time, Deb," Mike says.

"But who will I play with?" Deborah asks.

"You'll play with me," Nancy says. "A mommy-daughter adventure. Let Sam and Mike have some time together."

"Okay," Deborah says. She takes Nancy's hand and walks toward the pool, giving us a little wave over her shoulder. As they walk she keeps looking back. I wish we could have gone with her, but I'm also glad Mike chose to stay.

Once they are gone, Mike and I stand in silence. Awkward. Maybe I should take out my ball and bat. We're always best on the ball field. I'm about to suggest it when Mike says, "So, should we take a tour?"

Phew. I'm glad he spoke first.

"I'm not sure there's so much to see," I say. "But sure."

We stick to the tree line and walk by the trailers. Should I just come out and demand he tell me what's been going on or do I take the calmer, kinder approach?

"Can we sit?" he asks before I make up my mind. He points to a picnic table in one of the open campsites. I sit on the tabletop. He sits next to me. *This is it*, I think. He's going to tell me what's wrong. What I did.

But no, he stays silent. We can hear people laughing and yelling in the background, probably at the water park. Finally I can't take it anymore, "So what's up, Mike? What's with the silent treatment? I'm glad you seem to have forgiven me, but I still don't know what I did."

He takes in a deep breath and lets it out. "Look, I'm happy you made the travel team, I really am. Gabe read me the email so things should be better for you this year."

Wait, what?

"Gabe read you the email? Why didn't you read it yourself?"

He looks at me and suddenly I know why he's been upset. "You didn't make it? How is that possible? There must be a mistake."

"It's no mistake. They only had a few spots, remember? And they already had pitchers. The coach called and told my dad they'd still take me if they could, but only if they lose a player. I don't know why I blamed it on you. It's not like you were the last chosen. But somehow it felt like I would have gotten in if you didn't."

"Wow, I had no idea. I didn't even ask you because I assumed...I should have asked."

He shakes his head.

"So who can we get to move?" I ask as a joke. I think of the sign Tasha saw in front of my house. "Actually, you want to hear something crazy? For a few minutes there I thought it was going to be me."

"What do you mean?"

My fingers find my phone and I show him the picture of the For Sale sign.

"What's that? That can't be there."

"I know, right? Tasha saw it yesterday. Thankfully, I overheard Nancy talking about fixing the mistake they made at the house. So everything's good."

"They did that by mistake? That's a crazy mistake," Mike says.

He stands up and starts walking again. I follow.

"What?" I ask.

"You can't move, Sam." He takes my hand and looks into my eyes. Is he going to kiss me?

"We're not, I told you. It's a mistake. No worries, okay?"

He nods and leans in closer. My eyes close since that's what people do on TV. "Hey, hey you," a voice says, interrupting us. We move apart and look over to see a boy who looks around our age standing under an open pavilion.

"Us?" I ask.

"Him. Any chance you know how to play baseball?"

Mike gives me a look and shakes his head. He turns back to the boy. "Why?" he asks.

"We're having a game tonight, on the back lot that isn't being used." He points to an area by the road that's empty of tents and trailers. "It's not very fair. My fifteen-year-old brother Richie placed all the boys his age on one team and all the younger brothers on the other team."

"What about the girls?" I ask.

He laughs. "We aren't playing with *girls*. We're bad, but we're not *that* bad."

Mike opens his mouth, probably to tell this boy off, but I put my hand on his arm and stop him. "What's your name?" I ask.

"Oh, sorry. I'm Tommy."

"Tommy," Mike says, "I'd be happy to join your team but only if Sam can play too."

Tommy looks at Mike and then at me. "Why not?" he says. "We really couldn't be any worse. Just be careful," he tells me. "My brother throws them hard and I don't think he'll care that you're a girl."

Mike looks at me and gives a knowing smile.

We don't tell Tommy we're counting on it.

We leave for the field about ten minutes before 7:00 to check things out. Deborah insists on coming with us. We have no choice but to say yes when she puts on her Mets cap and grabs both of our gloves. Of course she's now wearing a puffy princess dress, but at least this one is Mets blue.

We decide not to bring our bats because it'll give us away.

"I'm a glove girl!" Deborah sings as we walk. "You're going to really show them, Sammy," she says when we reach the field.

"Shhhh," Mike and I say together.

"Right, secret," she says. She brings her fingers to her lips and pretends to lock them up and throw away the key.

The field isn't great, impressions of tents and RV wheels left over time make it bumpy and broken, but I've seen worse. There are marks that have recently been bases. Mike explores the mound. "What do you think?" I ask.

"It'll do," he says.

The voices of the boys reach us before we see them. They walk around an RV, talking and laughing. When they look up and see me, they stop dead in their tracks.

"This is your new player?" the boy who must be Richie says to Tommy. They both have the same red hair.

"Yeah, so?" Tommy answers.

"So, it's your team," Richie says with a chuckle. "Did you invite her baby sister too?" he asks, pointing to Deborah.

Mike steps up protectively. But instead of stepping forward and challenging the guy, he takes a step back and nods at me. My arms ache to give him a big hug but I settle for a quick, grateful nod. The last time the two of us were confronted like this at baseball camp he almost got into a fistfight. He's finally learned to trust I can handle it.

"Actually, my sister is a great hitter." A lie, but he doesn't have to know that. "But she's not dressed for baseball so you'll just have to settle for me."

"For us," Mike says.

"For us," I repeat.

"Fine," Richie says. "What do I care?" He laughs carelessly.

With that settled, the ten boys introduce themselves. Their ages stretch from a little younger than me to one guy who's sixteen. They came here from all over the country. Each one gives a look as they say hello. I bite my lip and shake my head.

"Don't worry about them," Tommy says. "You do the best you can. Do you need me to go over the rules?"

"That's okay," I say. This time Mike actually laughs out loud.

"What?" Tommy asks.

"You'll see," he says.

Mike volunteers to pitch and Tommy gladly takes him up on it. The fact that the teams are unbalanced is ridiculously obvious. Richie's team has five boys all around his age. With Mike, and me, Tommy's team now has seven, but everyone besides us is either our age our younger.

I'm not worried though, not if Mike's pitching.

Richie is first up to the plate. "Try not to hit me," he yells to Mike.

"I'm assuming that if I hit you, you get to take the base?" Mike says.

"Of course," Richie says.

"Then I won't hit you," Mike says.

He goes into his windup. "Strike him out, Mike!" Deborah calls. He gives her a nod and ends in the pitch. One, two, three…Richie is out before he knows the ball hasn't hit him.

"Hey! What the?" Richie says.

"Sorry, Richie," the catcher says. "They were all right over the plate."

"Well, lucky you," he says to Tommy. Tommy smiles at Mike and gives him a thumbs up. "Keep it going, man," he says.

"No problem," Mike says.

He strikes the next two batters out just as fast.

We run off the field. Richie gives Mike a look meant to melt him into the ground. Mike tips his hat at him instead. "Nice work," I whisper to him.

"Now it's your turn," Mike says to me.

Tommy announces the line-up. He places Mike third and me last, which means it could easily take three innings to get to the plate if everyone else strikes out. "Sam should switch with me," Mike says.

"Are you sure?" Tommy asks.

"Trust me," Mike says. "She's definitely the one you want."

"What, do you play softball or something?" Tommy asks.

"Or something," I say back.

Tommy's up first and strikes out. A boy named Ed is up next. He actually makes contact and gets onto first base, but only because one of the boys on Richie's team drops it.

Now it's my turn.

Tommy stops me. "Just give it a light tap and run as fast as you can. You'll probably get out, but hopefully Ed can get to second."

"Light tap, right," I said. I want to light tap them all on the side of their heads, but I smile anyway.

"Show them how to play like a girl," Mike whispers.

"I thought you always tell me to play like a guy," I whisper back.

"Not anymore," he says. He squeezes my arm.

"Tell the girl to stop talking to her boyfriend and get out here," Richie calls from the field. "Yeah, come on already," other voices add.

"Go, Sammy!" Deborah yells from the sidelines. She jumps up, claps, twirls, and hops. It almost looks like a cheer.

I pick up the bat and take a couple of shaky practice swings to get the feel of it. To anyone looking it will seem like I'm unsure, but really I'm checking balance and looking for any secrets. Usually the bat company has the sweet spot marked.

Richie, on the mound, shakes his head and smiles when I finally step up to the plate. "Okay, here comes the ball," he says.

My heart pounds. But I know I have nothing to lose. If I miss, they'd brush it off. And when I nail it…The moment brings me back to the last game with my home team—the last game I will play with Mike if he doesn't make Travel. How could he not have made Travel? It doesn't make sense. I see the ball whoosh toward me and take a stab at it, even though I know I'll miss. Mike probably thinks I did this on purpose, but really I'm in my own head. I breathe in and out to focus.

"It's okay, Sammy. Hit the next one!" Deborah calls. The other team howls, thinking she has no idea what she's talking about.

It's time to end the charade.

"Hey, Tommy," I call, correcting my stance and bending down into the plate. "Did I tell you what Mike and I did before we came here this summer?" My eyes find him over my shoulder but I'm really focusing on the pitcher. He's making a big deal of slowly winding up the pitch. Why do they all do that?

"No," Tommy says, "what did you do?"

I don't answer right away. Richie releases the ball. It comes at me in slow motion. My hands grip the bat tighter and I swing right into the pitch. My lips move into a smile as I make contact.

Crack! The ball sails over Richie's head, past the guy who's playing center. He had moved in, hoping to catch my hit if I managed to tap it. The ball continues and goes way out into the outfield, landing in some bushes. I watch it all from the plate, anticipating I'll have plenty of time to run once I see where it goes.

Leaving the bat at the plate, I run backwards toward first base to be sure Tommy and the rest of them hear me, "We went to baseball camp." I step on first base and run toward second. "And did I also forget to mention I just made Travel?" I say, stepping on second and running toward third. "Travel Baseball, by the way. The boys' team."

I've picked up too much speed to keep talking so I run around third and slide on my heel at home plate, just to show I can. Dusting myself off, I feel a grin take over my face. Some of the boys look upset but most on my team are laughing, especially Mike and Tommy.

Deborah does a small cartwheel. When'd she learn that?

When it's Mike's turn at bat, Richie asks, "So, are you in Travel too?"

Mike doesn't answer.

"He should be," I call.

Mike glares at me, then turns back to the pitch. What'd I do? Mike should be in Travel. It's so ridiculous that he's not.

We play for a few more innings. By now it's getting late. Dad comes to get Deborah and bring her back to the tent. She's so tired she jumps into his arms and lets him carry her back to the campsite.

By the end of the game Mike's let a couple get by him, but we field them easily. We win four to nothing.

"Nice game," Tommy says when it's all over.

"Thanks," I say.

"Do you need us to walk you back?" Tommy asks. I look at Mike and he shakes his head. "Are you sure?" Tommy says again. He's looking at me kinda funny.

"We're sure, thanks," Mike says firmly. He turns and heads back to our campsite without even a goodbye. He doesn't have to be rude.

"Well, maybe I'll see you around," Tommy says.

"Yeah, you never know," I answer.

THE PERFECT TRIP

It's full dark when we get back to our tent site. The adults sit around the fire, quietly talking. "Should we join them?" I ask Mike.

"I'm tired, actually," he says. "See you in the morning."

"See ya," I answer, not that we have a choice about that. "Great pitching tonight," I add.

"Thanks," he says flatly. He disappears inside his tent.

Dragging my feet, I reach my tent and step inside. Nancy follows me in.

"Did you have fun tonight?" she whispers. Deborah is sleeping on the air mattress again. Her little body takes up most of it.

"Yeah, I always love playing baseball. But you know, I do wish for once that the boys wouldn't assume from the start that I can't play. Will that ever change?"

Nancy shrugs. "When you do something very few people have done before you, there are bound to be challenges. But you have to define yourself by what you can do and not by what people think you can do."

"I know, but it's exhausting."

She nods. "And how are things with Mike?"

"Also exhausting," I answer.

She laughs. "I know what you mean. Boys. You're never quite sure what they're thinking, are you? I have that problem with your dad sometimes."

"But the two of you get along so well. I've never even seen you fight."

"We fight."

I give her a look, "About what?"

She pauses. "Lots of things," she says at last. "But relationships are like playing baseball, you have to know when to wait and when to swing."

Wow, Nancy's using baseball to make a point? I never thought I'd see this day.

"Hey, Nancy, get out here," my dad whispers loudly. Amy and Jim are laughing in the background.

"Have a good night, Sam," she says. She turns and heads back outside.

Before going to sleep I try to get in touch with Tasha, but my phone won't connect to anything.

The next morning we get up, eat breakfast, and take down the tents. As much as I'd love to play more baseball, I can't wait to leave this faux campground. Dad says the next place has a lake. Hopefully Nancy will let me swim.

But when we pull into the new campground, mosquitoes swarm the car.

"We can't stay here," Nancy says.

"What do you mean?"

"Jeff, if we have to take Sam to the Emergency Room again it will be the end of this trip. We are not staying here."

"But it's all paid for," Dad barks at her.

"I'll take care of it." She quickly opens and closes her door, trying to let in as few mosquitoes as possible.

Less than ten minutes later she's back in the car. She silently pulls her seatbelt over her shoulder.

"Well?" Dad asks at last.

"Here are the directions for a local motel. The man at the desk says it isn't all that nice but it was the best he could do."

"And the campsite?" Dad asks.

"Oh, he took off the charge."

My dad sits there, mouth open. "How?"

"After I threatened to sue him for our hospital fees, he was very accommodating," Nancy says. She stops talking, as if that says it all.

For a minute no one says anything. Then my dad laughs, setting all of us off. Every now and then Nancy reminds us that before she was a mom, she was a lawyer. I think Dad forgets too.

We say good-bye to Mike's family and drive to the motel. The guy at the campsite wasn't kidding, the place is a dump and makes the last one look like a palace. The stains on the rug, in the toilet, and in the shower look as old as the motel. But the screens work and it's mosquito free. Still, I'm expecting Nancy to have a meltdown. Instead she gets to work cleaning up.

"Sam, grab these sheets," she says. She quickly pulls them off the bed and replaces them with new ones she got from the office. Once the beds feel clean, Dad, Deborah, and I have a seat and try to teach Deborah to play Go Fish. Nancy places a blanket on a chair and plays on her phone.

Deborah falls asleep early and Nancy and Dad go outside again. I take out my phone to get in touch with Tasha. No service. But when I look for Wi-Fi and there's one unlocked! It can't be from this crappy hotel, so it's probably from the restaurant next door. Within seconds of connecting, my phone vibrates with incoming texts.

"Sam, where r u?"

"Sign still there."

"Leaving tomorrow."

"You can't move!"

Whoa. I check the time. It's only 10:30. Tasha's usually up pretty late. As soon as my text says delivered, I can see her responding.

"Sam! Sign's still there."

"Only been 2 days," I text back.

"Not sure. It's online."

What? She sends me the link to open in my Internet browser. The screen becomes clear and I'm looking at the outside of my house. It says the last time it was sold was 2010, which isn't right. It must be an old listing.

Clicking on the pictures to be sure, my stomach does a flip and I choke. There, on the screen, is my house set up the way it was when we left home. My signed bat is on the wall, though it looks like someone moved my trophies. Who would have touched my things? How can this be happening? My breath sticks in my throat and I feel faint.

"Well?" Tasha's text pops up, breaking into my paralysis.

"Don't know. Will find out."

"K, you betta," she writes back. "Only good thoughts."

My phone silences and I take a deep breath. Only good thoughts. I need to know what's going on. Should I run outside and confront them directly? But if they've been lying this whole time, they could lie now. I need to spy again. Crouching under the window, I pull back the curtain a bit so I can listen to their conversation.

"It's a good thing I was able to get him to give us back our money," Nancy says.

"Nancy, if we had to pay twice we would have been fine."

"But your job…"

This isn't at all the conversation I was expecting. My heart pounds. What is she saying, about his job? My neck aches as I stretch it closer.

"It will be fine, Nancy. I'm sure the new job will work out. My parents are looking into it."

"But what about Sam? She's so excited about Travel Baseball. She'll have to try out all over again, *if* she can try out."

They continue talking but I stop listening. My head is spinning. If Dad's talking about a new job, he's lost his old one. So this vacation is just a…lie? A way to avoid telling us Dad is out of work? No wonder he has the time off. The For Sale sign isn't a mistake. They really are selling the house. Without telling me.

I'm so angry I could spit. Stumbling to the bed, I pull the covers over my head, and face the truth. My dad, the one parent in my life who I've always counted on, has been lying to me. And all those weird looks from Nancy? She's wanted to tell me. That's what she meant by fighting with my dad. Nancy wanted to tell me, Dad is lying, and Travel isn't happening.

This is officially the worst trip ever.

I keep quiet all morning, not sure what to do next. Tasha already left for camp, so I can't reach her, and Mike is someplace with his family. I have to wait until we get to this place called Wisconsin Dells, where we are going on a boat trip. I'm so quiet, Nancy feels my head to make sure I'm not coming down with something. I can't even eat breakfast. When Deborah and Nancy finish, Nancy takes Deborah outside. As soon as they are out of sight I get Dad's attention.

"What is it, Sam?" he asks, as he gets out money to pay the bill. I pause, watching him. My dad's one of those guys who hands off his credit card without looking at the check. How can this be the first time I've noticed things are different?

"I need to use the bathroom," I say, leaving my questions unanswered. Once inside, I wash my face. It wasn't a dream. Dad's out of work.

There must be someone I can talk to. I pull out my phone and call my mom.

"Hello," she says.

"Mom?"

"Oh, Sam, is that really you. I've missed you. How's the trip so far?"

Not bothering to beat around the bush, I say, "We're moving."

"I know, honey. When did they tell you?"

She knows? They told her but they didn't tell me?

"They didn't tell me, I figured it out. Tasha saw the For Sale sign and I heard Dad and Nancy talking."

She laughs, which doesn't make me feel any better. "I told your father keeping it from you wouldn't work, but he never listens to me."

"How bad is it?"

She pauses. "Look, your Dad dug this hole so he's going to have to be the one to talk to you about it. It's about time he's the one you're mad at."

What does that mean, about time? I've never needed to be mad at Dad because he's been the one I've been able to trust. If I can't believe him, who's left?

"Thanks a lot," I say. I hang up the phone, wishing I hadn't called. She tries to call back but I don't answer.

Fear consumes me as we drive to the boat taking us around the Dells. How can we be out of money already? Wasn't he working last week? Could he have lost his job a long time ago and been lying to us? Thoughts race through my head and it barely registers when Nancy tells me she's pulling me from the riverboat if there are mosquitoes. I'd almost prefer staying in the car to being around these liars.

Nancy declares the boat dock mosquito free with a big smile. In a daze, I walk behind them. Nancy looks over at me a few times but before she can say anything, I go over and stand next to Mike. We haven't spoken since the end of the baseball game but I can't think about that now. When he looks at me, his eyes widen and I know he's figured out something is wrong.

"What is it?" he asks. "Your legs again?"

Shaking my head no, I take his hand to hopefully tell him he has nothing to do with my mood.

He gives my hand a squeeze, but doesn't ask me anything.

We head down the path, hand in hand. The boat is white and has two levels. Mike and I walk up the stairs and grab some seats in the front. Dad and Nancy stay with Deborah below. I sigh with relief.

"Is this about the moving sign?" Mike asks softly.

I nod.

"It wasn't a mistake."

I nod again. "And there's more. My dad's lost his job."

"What?" Mike says. "Are you sure?"

"I'm sure."

Mike doesn't say anything else, but his grip on my hand tightens. People sit around us, but it's like we're in our own private space. Him and me, in this together, at least for the moment. The boat pulls out and we're surrounded by rocky cliffs. I'd admire their beauty if I weren't so upset.

A voice speaks on the loudspeaker.

"Welcome to the tour of the Upper Wisconsin Dells. This area is called Wisconsin Dells because Wisconsin means 'dark rushing river' and Dells means collections of flat plates of rock. As we travel down the river you will get a chance to see rocks dating back over 500 million years."

"Dad, is that a long time?" I hear Deborah ask. I look up and spot them sitting on this level, close to the middle of the boat.

"Long enough that dinosaurs weren't even on the earth," Dad answers.

"You mean after they died out?" Deborah asks.

"No, I mean before they were even born," Dad says.

I can't imagine a time before the dinosaurs. I take a glance at Dad. He always knows everything about, well, everything. How could he not have planned for something like a lost job?

The boat continues. We come to a spot where the rocks seem to reach in.

"This spot is called the gateway to the Upper Dells. Once we pass this point we will see places of lumberjacks, witches, and Indians," the tour guide continues.

We travel on past different rock formations. As we came around the next bend I think I see someone's nose carved out of rock. Great, so now I'm hallucinating.

"Do you see that?" Mike asks me.

Oh, thank goodness. It's not just me. "It looks like a face," I answer. "Is it a statue?"

The loud speaker answers, "On your right you will see Blackhawk Rock. It was named for the Indian Chief, Blackhawk. He was said to have hidden on Blackhawk Island, which we passed a few minutes ago."

"Who do you think he was hiding from?" I ask Mike. Maybe his parents?

Mike actually answers, "Blackhawk was an Indian chief in the 1800s. He fought, and lost, a war against the settlers in this area. The war was named after him."

"Wow," I said. "How do you know that?"

"I tried to read as much as I could about all the places we were going to visit."

"That's cool," I tell him.

He smiles.

The rocks bend inwards, coming closer on both sides. It almost seems like the river is going to be blocked completely.

"This area is called the Narrows," the voice calls.

"Good name," Deborah calls out.

We travel through the Narrows and past even tighter areas called "Devil's Elbow" and "Steamboat Rock." It's unbelievable how close we are to the sides of the canyon. If I reach out, I can touch them.

The boat stops at a place called "Witches' Gulch."

"Eek, witches," Deborah says. She comes over to Mike and me. "Do you think they're still here?"

"Don't be silly, Deb," I say. "There are no witches."

"But if you are worried, Sam and I can hold your hands," Mike says.

She nods.

The boat docks and we get off and walk on stone pathways lined with wood railings. The pathways weave in and out of the rocks. They are so close at times Dad needs to duck. I hope he hits his head.

"Wow, it's a good thing none of us are claustrophobic," Amy says.

"What's clauster-fo-bick?" Deborah asks us.

"It means getting scared in small, tight, places," I answer.

"Oh, why would *that* make you scared? Witches are scary, not rocks."

Right now the only thing that's scaring me is the thought of moving. Well, that, and Dad lying to me.

We walk around for a while, then get back on the boat. It pulls out and continues down the river.

"Our next stop is Stand Rock," the voice announces.

"Okay, guys, this is it. The thing I've been waiting for," Dad says.

"Why? What's so special about Stand Rock?" Deborah asks.

"You'll see," he says mysteriously. I roll my eyes.

We disembark from the boat again and go up another windy path. As we get closer, our eyes meet an incredible sight. A pillar of rock stands by itself a few feet from the edge of a cliff. Almost too tall to see, its top is wide and flat and looks like a large stone table for a giant.

"Daddy, there's a dog up there!" Deborah says. I look closer and see it too. I point it out to Mike.

"How'd it get up there?" Mike asks.

"What are they doing with a dog?" Deborah adds.

"You'll see," Dad says again.

Deborah turns to me. "Sammy, what are they going to do with that dog?"

"It looks to me like they are going to make him jump over to the other rock," I tell her. That's the only thing that would make sense to me.

Deborah grabs my thigh. "Why, Sammy? Why would they do that? What if the dog falls?"

"He's not going to fall, Deb," I say. He'd better not. It's a long way to the ground.

"Mommy," Deborah says. "Make them stop. I don't want to see the dog fall." Tears are starting to drip down the corner of her eyes. Nancy is standing with Amy and doesn't hear her. I hold Deborah's shoulders to make her feel safe.

At that moment the dog jumps. Deborah whips her body around and buries her face in my stomach. Her whole body trembles. The dog lands, gracefully, on the other side.

"He made it, Deb," I say. "The dog is fine."

"Are you sure?" she asks quietly.

The dog turns around and leaps back across to the other side. Everyone claps. It's amazing.

"I'm sure. Look, look up and see for yourself," I say.

Placing her chin in my hand, I slowly turn her face up to see the dog standing happily back on the cliff.

"Who'd like to see it again?" the announcer asks.

Deborah shudders.

"Nancy, Deborah and I are going back to the dock," I say.

She waves us away, too fascinated by the dog to look over.

"I'll come with you," Mike says.

Deborah's grip on my hand has made my fingers numb, but I don't let go. Protecting her reminds me of the talk Dad and I had before we left Connecticut. He told me I would need to watch out for her. His exact words were, "We have a lot of changes coming soon and she'll need her big sister to look out for her."

At the time I thought he was talking about being on a trip in the woods, but he must have been talking about moving. She's so much younger than me. Will that make moving harder or easier? I have to stop freaking out and be strong about this, like that dog jumping across cliffs. But first I have to understand what's going on.

It's time to get Dad and Nancy to tell the truth.

13

We get back into the car and head toward the next campground. Deborah wants a Princess story, but I tell her she's too tired. I'm right. With all the excitement with the dog she's out in minutes, giving me time to think. Should I come straight out and tell Dad and Nancy I know about the job and the move? Or maybe I should talk to Nancy alone since I'm pretty sure she's almost told me a few times.

But this is my dad, the guy who tells me everything. Lying is what my mom is known for, not him.

When we get to the next campsite my eyes light up. It's everything I look for: trees, privacy, and there's definitely a lake. No way this place isn't mosquito heaven.

I expect Nancy to immediately turn around and head to the hotel. But when she comes back to the car she's smiling ear to ear. "They spray," she says.

"The whole site has been mosquito bombed so it should be fine."

Torn between this perfect campground and the chance to have a private conversation I ask, "Are you sure?"

"I'm sure. Even a tent is cleaner than the motel we stayed in last night and I know how much you have missed being outside. You've been so unhappy."

If only my problem has been the motel.

We put up the tent, much quicker this time. Nancy and Deborah even help. One happy family.

"Have you talked to them yet?" Mike asks when both tents are up.

Shaking my head, I say, "Not yet."

"No better time than now," he says, pointing me toward my dad.

Dad's standing by the fire, talking to Jim. As I approach, the odor of burnt wood tickles my nose.

Jim nods to me and my dad turns around. "Sam?" he asks.

"Dad, can we go for a walk?" I ask.

"I don't see why not. What do you think, Jim?"

Jim looks at me and raises his eyes. "Did you want us all to come along?" he asks. The expression on his face reminds me so much of Mike's.

"Actually, Dad, I'd like to take a walk alone. With you."

"Of course, Sam. I always have time for my Cracker Jack."

He says bye to Jim and we head for the lake. The greenery is so thick Dad has to hold branches high so I can walk through without being smacked. We push through the last section and the lake opens up before us like an unfolding flower. A hazy mist of dirt and bugs lines its shores. At the far edge, a hill seems to rise straight out of the water and the trees on riverbanks bend forward as if they are trying to see their reflection in its surface.

"Did I ever show you how to skip rocks?" Dad asks, breaking into the silence.

"I think so," I say. I have a vague memory of standing by a lake with Mom and Dad, and him showing me how to do it, but it was a long time ago. "Can you show me again?"

He looks around in the mud and finds a couple of small stones. He hands one to me and I toss it in the water. Plunk! It sinks below the surface.

"You can't throw a rock like you throw a baseball. It's more like throwing a Frisbee. More wrist than arm."

He demonstrates and the rock makes three skips before disappearing under the surface. He hands me another one. This time I imagine throwing the ball to first base side arm. I get two skips.

"Not bad," he says. "See, your old man is still good for something."

The way he says it is so sad. But I have to talk to him.

"Dad," I start.

He sniffs a couple times, his body positioned away from me, facing the trees. His shoulders are moving up and down. Is he crying? Dad never cries, ever.

Feeling awkward, I pick up a few more rocks and practice skipping them. My fourth one skips five times!

"I knew you could do it," Dad says. His voice is solid now. His sudden despair left him faster than it came. I breathe a sigh of relief. Seeing him cry is almost worse than knowing we have to move.

"Do you want to walk back?" I ask.

He peers at me for a moment, tilting his head. "If that's what you want," he says. He doesn't ask me if I'm okay or anything else. Maybe he doesn't want to know.

We traipse back through the undergrowth, faster this time. Dad heads over to Jim, who is trying to start a fire. Nancy and Amy are getting chicken ready as Deborah twirls around.

Mike makes a beeline for me. "Well?" he asks.

I shrug.

He gives me the same look that I saw on his dad's face. The *I-know-there's-something-you're-not-telling me-look*.

"Want to play some ball?" Mike asks. I nod. He always knows how to cheer me up.

"Can I play?" Deborah asks. My mouth hangs open. I've tried to teach her a number of times, but she's never done it willingly.

"Absolutely," I say.

She runs inside and changes into shorts and her Mets hat. Scanning the area, I find a good spot where the bushes are tight together and should block any missed balls. "You pitch and I'll catch," I tell Mike.

"Of course," he says.

"Okay, Deb," I say when she comes back. "Stand right here."

The bat I brought, which is one of my favorites, is completely wrong for her size, but there's nothing I can do about that now. We'll have to do the best we can. She tries to grab it from me. I shake my head and put it on the ground instead.

"Not yet," I tell her. "We have work to do first. Show me a fist."

She looks at me through slatted eyes, but goes along with it, holding up her right hand with her fingers clenched. "That's great. Now make another fist."

With a bit more enthusiasm this time, she takes the other hand and holds it next to the first.

"Am I punching something?" she asks.

"You're practicing holding a bat. Now put your two fists together, one on top of the other." Holding out my own hands, I demonstrate. She copies me easily. "See how all of your fingers are now in a row?"

"But some are on one side and some are on the other."

"That's okay. Look at your knuckles and the places your fingers bend." I point them out to her. "See how they're all lined up? That's what you want to see when you hold a bat. Watch." I pick up the bat and show her how my fingers are all together. "Now you try it."

She takes the bat and squeezes her hands so hard they start looking red. "Not so tight. You don't need to smush the bat, just hold it." She nods and releases her grip a little. The bat dips a bit because it's so big and heavy compared to her size.

"Now we'll practice standing and swinging."

Any minute I think she'll say she's bored and stop playing, but she surprises me. I demonstrate my stance and how to swing the bat. She follows my movements the best she can and allows me to lightly move her into better positions. Finally, Mike throws her some balls, using tennis balls instead of baseballs so they are lighter. He pitches it straight at the bat. When it makes contact and bounces away, she jumps up and down and screams, "I did it, Sammy. You're a great teacher."

I give her a hug. She's very wobbly, but it's a very good start. Amy and Nancy join us as fans, cheering for every hit ball, even when it bounces off the bat and lands close to Deborah's feet.

We take a quick dinner break, then play until dusk. Hints of pink and purple filter through the trees by the lake.

"Can Mike and I go watch the sunset?" I ask Nancy.

"Me too!" Deborah says.

"Not this time," Nancy says. "Sam and Mike have played with you all afternoon. And it's time for your book and bedtime."

"Awww," she says, but she goes into the tent willingly.

I mouth, "Thanks," to Nancy. She sends me a smile and points me forward with her chin before disappearing inside after Deborah.

Mike follows me down the path to the lake. I hold the branches for him.

"So?" he asks when we get to the edge of the water.

"He cried, Mike, real tears. I couldn't ask him. Besides, what's the point of asking? I already know the answer."

"But aren't you curious why this happened so fast? I am."

"Does it matter? Either way, we're moving. And at least this means you'll make the team."

"You know I don't care about that," he says. He takes a step closer and holds my hand. Now I feel like I'm going to cry.

"You should care, Mike. You're an awesome player and deserve it. At least if I'm moving, you get that chance."

"They still might not take me because you aren't a pitcher. And what about you, Sam? They've probably finished tryouts in Wyoming, if they even have a team. How are you going to play?"

"No idea. But if Dad's not going to tell me anything, I guess I'll have to figure that out."

It's gotten dark. We can hear all sorts of animals in the trees. Mike comes closer and puts his hand on my cheek. This time there's no one to interrupt us. No one but me.

Placing my hand over his, I gently lead it away from my face. "Mike, I'm moving," I say.

"I know that," he says. He moves to replace his hand. I take it again and hold it in place.

"I just need a friend right now. Okay?"

Please let it be okay.

He hesitates and opens his mouth, possibly to argue, but his eyes catch mine and soften. He pulls me into a strong hug instead.

In the morning we pack up the tents and head out. The adults are being funny this morning, none of them telling us where we are going. I'm quiet again, but not because I'm sad, because I'm plotting. If we are going to move, I have to be ready. Mike's right. I can't stop playing baseball because of this. I have to find a way to make the team. Hopefully, wherever we are going today has cell service or Wi-Fi.

We pull off the highway and come to a city. Most of the buildings are short, but we can see one in the distance, which makes me forget baseball for the moment. I can clearly see Arabian turrets. In South Dakota? They're completely out of place. As we get closer I notice flags line the sides of the building and all around are murals made out of tiny yellow, black, and brown stones.

"It's a castle!" Deborah exclaims. She reaches into her bag and quickly pulls out her crown and places it around her curls.

"Not a castle," Dad says. "A palace! A Corn Palace!"

Corn? It's made of corn? Dad talked about this place when he told us about the trip, but this wasn't exactly what I was expecting. In my Princess Deborah story I made the Corn Palace a small place, like an American Indian wigwam. This building is huge.

"The whole thing can't be made of corn. It would spoil," I say. "And there are bricks at the bottom."

"And bird's would eat it. Wouldn't they, Mommy?" Deborah added.

Nancy smiles and lets Dad answer.

"No, yes, and yes," Dad says. "It is not made of corn, it's covered in corn. But the corn does spoil and birds do eat it."

"It doesn't look broken," I say. My brow wrinkles. There must be some answer. Suddenly I have it.

"They rebuild it?" I ask.

"Every year," Dad says, smiling. "It's a monument to starting over and trying something new."

He would say that. We park the car and go closer. I see a big FREE sign by the door and wonder if that was what had attracted my dad to this place, but he's bouncing around with Mike's parents and examining each mural. This is definitely on his list of must-sees.

Considering how excited Dad is, I'm expecting to see something truly special inside the palace as well, like rooms and furniture made of corn, but inside's a large room that looks like my school gym.

"Hmm," Dad says, looking around.

Jim says, "It looks like there's some sort of concert in an hour. Do you want to stay?"

Mike gives me a look. If I can find a computer or Wi-Fi, I'm all for it.

"Can we explore?" I ask them.

"Sure, why not? Just come back here when you're done," Jim says.

We move to the side of the room, over to some cases on the wall. Inside are pictures of all the different ways the Corn Palace has been decorated over the years. I point it out to Dad and Jim and they gather up Nancy, Deborah, and Amy to take a look. Between this and the concert, I should have plenty of time to do some research.

"Come on," I say to Mike.

We leave the main room and find a side hallway. No computer lab, but when I check my phone there's full service and Wi-Fi. I plop down on a bench to begin my search.

"What are we looking for?" Mike asks.

"Travel teams in Wyoming," I answer. And maybe a clue of how they feel about girls playing ball.

Mike takes out his phone too and we both search. I find the website for the town teams and it says they have baseball up to the age of 18, but there's no information about how to sign up for anything for kids over 12.

"You find anything?" I ask Mike.

He shakes his head no.

"I tried girls baseball Wyoming and saw some photos of younger girls who play, but nothing about where."

This bites. If I figured this out myself, I wouldn't have to bother Dad and Nancy, and I wouldn't have to see him cry again. But that's not going to happen.

Finding a contact link, I send an email to the person in charge of the team site and hope for the best.

"Maybe you can talk to your dad?" Mike says.

"We've already gone over that," I say. He shrugs.

We find Deborah and our parents in the gift shop. Amy buys corn for us to cook tonight. "Are you sure you don't want us to get it?" Nancy asks her.

"Oh, no, it's corn. It's on us," Amy says. She places her hand on Nancy's arm and Mike and I give each other a look. His parents definitely know.

"Over here, Sammy, over here," Deborah calls from three giant corn stalks with holes cut out for heads.

"Oh, no," I say.

"Come on, might as well have some fun," Mike says.

He takes my hand and pulls me over to the corn. We take a number of shots with silly faces. Deborah begs us for one smiling shot and I do my best not to let her down. Will the dance programs in Wyoming be as good as the ones Deborah belongs to now?

Dad and Nancy haven't really thought this all through.

"That was not quite what I expected," Dad says as we go back to our car. "But it was still fun, don't you think?"

"I loved it!" Deborah says. "And the corn was yummy."

"If you think that was interesting, wait till you see what's in store for you next!" Dad says.

How can he say that with a straight face when the thing in store for us is moving?

15

I stay quiet for most of the ride. Deborah asks for a new Princess story but I tell her I feel carsick. Nancy starts to give me *the look*, but pulls it back when she sees my face. I *am* sick, just not from the car. Deborah falls asleep instead.

Dad wakes her up a few hours into the drive. "We are now going to enter...*the Badlands*," he says in a spooky voice usually reserved for Halloween and ghost stories. A tingle goes up and down my spine.

"The Badlands? What makes them bad?" Deborah asks, rubbing her eyes.

Dad doesn't answer. Instead he starts humming, leaving us to our own imagination. I don't know why he doesn't know that kind of thing never works for Deborah. Then again, at the moment he doesn't seem to know what would be good for me either.

As I knew would happen, Deborah's eyes are wide and she keeps looking back and forth. "What's wrong?" I ask.

"Sammy, do you think bad means scary?" she asks.

"Deb," I say, "the only bad things that happened in this area happened a long time ago."

"Like cowboys chasing Indians?" she asks.

"Yes, but if you see an American Indian now they won't look any different than you or me. That is, unless they're in traditional dress celebrating a holiday."

She exhales. "Good," she says. "Because the first person captured is always the princess." She smiles and adjusts her crown.

Giving her my best smile, I push back my feelings about Wyoming. My plan to be strong for Deborah will be much harder if I can't play baseball at all. And Dad may be excited about this place, but so far all I see is dry and rough ground and rolled hay. "This area is probably called the Badlands because no one would ever want to live here."

"Actually you aren't so far off, Sam," Dad says. "It was named Badlands because of the lack of water. Fur trappers didn't like coming into the area because it was hard to survive."

"Fur trappers?" Deborah asks.

"You know, people who killed animals for their fur," I say.

She thinks for a moment. "Well, it was *the Good Lands* for the animals then, huh?"

Nancy laughs and I give Deborah's leg a loving squeeze. She can always find a positive way to look at things. Sometimes I wish I were four.

We drive on and the land out my window changes. The flat land seems like it drops off into cliffs that look like pictures I've seen of the Grand Canyon with grayish layered rock. Others look like the sand dunes you find on a golf course.

"Are you seeing this?" Mike texts me. He sends a picture of one of the more obvious drops.

We pull into a ticket booth and pay. Nancy sighs as she hands Dad the money and he stares her down. A second later he smiles as if nothing happened. "This is going to be worth it, you'll see."

She looks back out her window and presses her forehead on the glass to see out further. She probably thinks this is another disappointment.

The ridge on our left is getting deeper. Nancy's phone buzzes.

"Amy says a scenic overlook is coming up and they're pulling off," Nancy tells Dad.

"What does that mean?" Deborah whispers to me.

"It means a place where we can get a closer look at this area," I answered.

"Ohhh," she says.

We follow Mike's car into the rest area, park, and get out. From where we stand we can see miles of rock cut cliffs. They're jagged and smooth at the same time. It looks like a giant child playing on a beach dug them out of the earth. Thinking back to the pillar we saw in Wisconsin, the one the dog jumped onto, maybe giants made this whole country originally. If Dad had turned to me at that moment and told me they had, I would have believed him. Or the way things stand, maybe not.

Dad points to a place where the land jets out over the canyon. "Okay, everyone, let's get out there and take a picture," Dad says.

"Jeff, you're crazy. There aren't any rails out there," Nancy says.

Dad hands her his phone. "Why don't you take the picture if you're worried?"

He signals Mike's dad and grabs our hands. We walk out on the rock. There's plenty of space to stand, but Nancy's still panicked.

"Jeff, be careful. It looks like you're going to fall right over the edge."

"It's fine, Nancy," Dad says. "Stop worrying."

"One of us needs to worry," Nancy calls back.

"It's perfectly safe," Jim calls to her, cutting off their back and forth. "You should come out and give the camera to someone else to hold."

"But," she starts to argue. But she must have realized it's hopeless because she holds the camera up and takes the picture.

"Okay, it's done. Now come back to the car and stop giving me a heart attack."

We laugh, but Nancy's not smiling.

We climb into the car and take off again. The road continues to loop around. From my window I can see that the area with the rocks is pretty large. It seems to grow as I look back.

"Are there more?" Deborah asks. "I can't see!"

"Don't worry, there's more," Dad says.

Deborah starts pulling and twisting in her booster seat. There better be more soon.

"Can I let her sit on my lap?" I ask.

"Sure," Nancy says, "Let's get everyone killed. Then we have nothing to worry about."

It's so untypical for Nancy, I don't know what to say. But I don't get Deborah out of her seat.

Finally the land starts noticeably changing next to the car, not just in the distance. We can see the tips of the hills, no longer as cliffs but as larger mounds. There are so many shapes and sizes. It reminds me of times I've been at the beach, when I've taken wet sand and let it pour slowly out of the edge of my hand. I remind Deborah of that experience.

"Oh yeah," she says. "So whose hand made these?"

I want to tell her about the image of the giant I have in my head, but it may scare her. Instead I say, "Whoever they were, they had really big hands."

She nods.

We come to another scenic overlook. Nancy doesn't argue but waves of disappointment steam off her like gas. There's no drop at this one so we think we're safe. I stand next to Mike, looking out. "Where do these come from?" I ask aloud, not really expecting an answer.

"Actually, it's kinda cool," Mike says. "Each layer we see is made by things that happened in this area. For instance, that dark color is ash from volcanoes that erupted 30 million years ago. Whereas that other dark color is from mud that was at the bottom of an ocean that covered this area 75 million years ago. It's like we are looking at the history of the world."

I look at Mike with a newfound respect. It's one thing for him to do research about who lived in the Wisconsin Dells. This goes beyond that. It's not like I don't know Mike's smart, we're in the same advanced classes at school, but he doesn't usually show off that guy.

"That's pretty cool," I tell him. "What else?"

He points at another layer of rock. That's when Deborah gives a yell.

"Mommy, what does that sign say?" she asks.

We all look over and read the sign she's talking about. It has a big picture of a rattlesnake.

"It says we're getting back in the car without arguing," Nancy demands.

Mike gives me a wink and gets back into his car. My heart does a little flutter. After all these years of only knowing the baseball guy he's finally showing me more. Right in time for me to move.

We continue to look at the layers as we pass through hills, which keep growing in size. Dad tries to convince Nancy to get out and walk around again, but she's not having it. She just shakes her head and continues looking out her window. We drive on.

What else would I learn about Mike if we had more time together? I've known him for practically my whole life. Why did he wait until now to show me this side?

As suddenly as the raised cliffs began, they end. What's left are little white rock mounds that remind me of sand traps on a golf course. Each time I think they're gone I look out on another section of cliff. As we continue, the breaks in the land get less frequent until there's just land.

Deborah points out her window and says, "Look, Sam, cows!"

I look out her side. For as far as I can see there are bison, acres of bison. Each beast is enormous with its large furry head and skinny legs.

"They're so big!" Deborah exclaims.

They are big, and coming right for us. "Dad," I yell. "They're coming across the road."

He looks out his window and slams on the breaks. Mike's car has already gone ahead but they stop and get out to watch. In a moment a herd is crossing right in between our two cars. Dirt churns the air and the smell of manure and dust surrounds us.

There are so many of them it's hard to imagine they'll ever go by us. And it's so loud. "Come on!" Dad yells. He waves us outside so we can get a better look. Nancy shakes her head and puts on earphones. We leave her behind.

After what seems like forever, the last ones finally pass. We follow behind them a little, walking into the field.

"A big, happy family," Dad says.

If only that were true of us as well.

"Go away! Jeff, help, make it go away!" we hear from behind us.

We turn around and look back at the car. A donkey stands at Nancy's window. We can see its tail swishing but its head is in the car.

"Get out! Go away!" Nancy shouts over and over again.

Mike and his parents are closest so they rush over to the car to try to scare the animal away. I turn to run over too, but I notice Dad isn't coming. His head is down and his whole body is shaking.

"Dad, are you okay?" I ask. Did it all finally get to him?

He looks up. Water pours from his eyes, but he is smiling. The shaking is laughter. He's laughing so hard he can barely breathe.

"Is Daddy okay?" Deborah asks.

"He's fine, he's just laughing," I answer.

"Not nice, Daddy," Deborah reprimands.

The two of us run back to the car to help. I go to an empty window and look inside. The donkey's head is in Nancy's lap and it's busy eating our snack! Mike and Jim are trying to push and yell at it, but it isn't going anywhere.

"Nancy, throw some of the snack out the window, then roll the window up as soon as the donkey moves away," I say.

"Okay," she says. She takes a handful of pretzels and dumps them outside. The donkey follows the food. Nancy hands me the bag and I make a path away from the car and dump the rest on the ground.

"Thanks for your help," Nancy says to Dad as he sits down.

Dad cracks up again. "Nancy, it was a donkey, not a bear."

Nancy looks away.

We pull out behind Mike's car. There's something unspoken between Nancy and Dad that goes beyond a donkey. I'm sure it has to do with moving and the job. Why can't they just get it out in the open?

"So? Better than the Corn Palace?" Dad says as he regains his composure.

"Pretty amazing," Deborah says.

"And that's not even half as special as the place we are going tomorrow," Dad says.

We all groan, though probably not all for the same reasons.

16

The Badlands turn into green covered hills and mountains. Dad tries to engage Nancy and me, but neither of us is up for talking. Instead, he talks to Deborah.

"I think you will like this next place, Deb," Dad says.

"Why, Daddy?" she asks.

"You'll see," he says. I'm getting really tired of his "you'll sees." And if Deborah will like it, I'm guessing I won't. If it's another boring, over-marketed, water park campground, I don't think I can take it.

We stop for dinner and then continue the trip to the campsite. The first thing I see is a large flat parking lot. I sigh but we keep going. We pass through a wide area designated for trailers that seems to go on for miles. I sink down lower.

But once the trailers are behind us, we enter true forest. A dirt road leads away from a log cabin. Tents are tucked in and out of the trees. There's also an area with small log cabins and a number of fire pits.

"Daddy, are those mountains?" Deborah asks, pointing into the distance, through the trees.

"Well, they call them the Black Hills, but they certainly are tall, aren't they?" Dad answers.

My hands open the car door and I step outside to get a better view. They are pretty spectacular. Covered with evergreens like a carpet, they rise high into the sky on all sides of the campground. I'll have to ask Mike later where they got that name. I bet he'll know.

We get out and join Mike's family at the log cabin. There's a list of activities posted that includes nighttime events such as wagon rides and barbecues.

How can we afford this? is the first thing that jumps into my mind. Even if we are staying in a tent, a place like this has to be expensive. *Let them worry about it,* I order myself. After all, they haven't even told me he lost his job. It isn't my problem.

"We'll hang out here," I tell the adults. They go inside. Mike comes close to me and grabs my hand. "How are you doing?" he asks.

I shrug and follow Deborah along a wooden fence. Mike walks next to me. Deborah is wearing a silver crown for the occasion. The railing ends at an open gate in front of a large enclosure to the side of the store.

"Have you talked to your dad?" Mike whispers, once Deborah is a few feet away.

"I told you, I can't. It'll make him too upset. Plus he's having this fight with Nancy."

"So what?"

I can't explain it in a way that makes sense. My dad has always been my rock, the one who stayed when my mom flaked out. The one who stood by me when I felt alone and who at least tried to make things okay when he married Nancy. Seeing him cry broke my heart more than the idea of moving. And seeing him and Nancy fighting isn't making things better. When I hated her and wanted them to fight, they didn't. So why now?

Mike takes my silence as an answer. "I think you're being..."

His words are cut off by rumbling. The ground is shaking. Is it an earthquake? More bison? We need to get Deborah to cover. But, shoot, where *is* Deborah?

Her voice shouts above the thunderous sound, helping me find her. "Horses!" she screams with glee. "Sammy, look at all the horses!"

Her finger points across a large field. She's right. The sound is horses. They move swiftly, one trying to outrun the next. I count eight of them, all different colors, with manes blowing behind them, and they're coming straight for an opening to a big corral, the opening in which Deborah is currently standing.

"Deb!" I yell. "Move!"

"Look, Sammy, my horse is coming! It's Misty, the gray horse that belongs to Princess Deborah. Look!" Instead of running, she puts up her hand to stop the horses, just like Princess Deborah did in my story. These horses aren't going to stop.

Mike and I take off at the same time. My senses tell me they're getting closer but I don't look. Instead I imagine I'm running around the bases, trying to get to home before being tagged out. The ground's bumping and roaring with the horses' footsteps.

Reaching Deborah, I scoop her up in my arms as if I'm retrieving a ball from the ground. In the same motion I keep moving until I'm past the gate. Mike runs next to us, screaming at the horses to stop and protecting us with his body.

"Put me down, Sammy," Deborah yells. "I want to see my horse!" She pounds on my shoulders. I've just saved her life and she's mad? Sisters!

"Deb," I say in her ear, "if I put you down will you stay here, holding my hand?"

"I promise," she says.

My arms shake as I put her back down. She takes my hand and Mike grabs her other one. She isn't moving until we let her.

By now the horses have slowed down. The sound is no longer deafening. Men on horseback follow the horses into the pen and work on settling them down. Where were they earlier? The horses finally slow to a trot and we can hear again.

"You didn't let me use my horse stopping power," Deborah says.

"Deb, Princess Deborah is a story. This is real life. Those horses would have run you over."

"Oh, Sammy, you're so silly sometimes," she says. "If you want it enough, stories become real. Like the tooth fairy."

I don't know what to say to that.

"Sam! Deborah!" Dad yells from the store steps.

"We're over here," Mike yells.

"Oh, look at all the horses!" Amy says as she walks up. "I didn't see them here when we went inside."

"Not only are there horses," Dad says, "but tomorrow night we are going to ride them out into the woods and have a real cowboy cookout."

Deborah claps her hands. I groan.

We get back into the car and drive down a long dirt road. My heart is still thumping in my chest as loud as those horses' hoofs were pounding on the ground, yet Deborah is all smiles thinking about riding those horses.

"What's going on with you, Sam?" Dad asks. "This is your dream campground yet you still look miserable."

"Maybe you would like to talk to Sam about this privately?" Nancy asks.

"No, we're all family here. And I think we all deserve to know why Sam's been upset."

Nancy gives him *the look*, the one that is usually reserved for me.

"What?" Dad says.

"Why has Nancy been upset?" I snap back.

"You know why Nancy's upset. We're on a camping trip, I took you into a dangerous spot, and a donkey put his head in her lap."

It would be funny if I wasn't so mad. "And that's the only reason?" I push.

They look at each other. Well, Dad looks, Nancy glares. "Isn't that enough?" Dad asks.

"I'm going to go back to the washroom to change," Nancy says. "I still smell like donkey."

She gets out of the car and looks around. "Where's the bathroom?"

Dad pulls out the map. "It looks like there are bathrooms over by the main building."

"But that was way over there. What do we do over here?" Nancy asks.

"There's always the woods," Dad says.

Nancy flashes him an even stronger look, one I've actually never seen. "I'm *not* using the woods," she says.

"Well, what would you like me to do?" Dad asks.

"I would like you to go back there and tell him we need a closer site," Nancy says. "But I guess I'll have to do it."

Nancy has worked miracles before, but this place is packed. I don't think there are any campsites left.

Nancy marches back to the store anyway. Amy goes with her. Mike and I sit on a bench waiting while Jim and my dad whisper in the corner. Mike looks at me to say something, but I put up my hand. "Don't even," I say.

Deborah comes over and sits between us. She takes both of our hands. I don't think she's ever seen her parents fight. Nancy and Amy come back a while later but their steps have a lot less bounce.

"Nothing," Nancy says. "The only campsites left are even further away."

"It will be fine, Nancy," Dad says softly. "You'll see."

At exactly that moment a bolt of lightning sails across the sky.

Mike, Amy, and Jim put their tent up in seconds, then they come over to help us with ours. Nancy and Deborah stay in the car. Just as we add an extra tarp to the roof the skies open up and it pours. Not a little drip either, but enough rain to make it nearly impossible to see outside.

"Great," Nancy calls. "This is just great."

"Mommy," Deborah whines loud enough to hear, "I have to go pee-pee!"

Nancy sighs and shakes her head. She moves around the car and finds umbrellas and rain jackets. She also pulls out a pair of rain boots for Deborah.

"Okay, Deb, come with me," she says once every part of her body has been covered, buttoned, and zipped. "We may stay there a while, do you want to come?" she asks me.

No, I shake. I'm soaked through and would rather change here. I watch them leave then go inside the tent. Dad's in a mood. He puts on his rain coat, then leaves to borrow Mike's family's charger so he doesn't have to blow up the air mattress outside. I take off my wet things, change into comfortable clothes, and climb into my sleeping bag.

Dad's still not back so I do a quick phone check. We have service! I open Mail and right at the top there's an email from the baseball woman in Wyoming. I quickly open it and sigh with relief. I can still try out! I'm so thankful I feel like I'm going to cry. Finally some good news!

Dad gets back and blows up the mattress. He carefully places Nancy's bag next to Deborah's, then he places his own bag closer to me. This really isn't good. I don't remember much about my parent's divorce, but I know it started with little things like this. I wish I could talk to Tasha. Dad finally finishes and sits on his bag and faces me.

"Everything's fine," he says. But his tone sounds to me like he's trying to convince himself.

I shrug, not sure what he wants me to say. We sit in silence for a few minutes listening to the rain.

"You seem a bit happier now, Sam. So now can you tell why you aren't more excited about the horses?" Dad asks. "I really thought you would think this place was great."

"I do think it's great." Especially now that I don't have to worry about a team. "But I'm not sure about the horses. They're crazy."

"What do you mean?"

"Before you came outside they almost ran over Deborah. I had to run and pick her up before she was trampled."

"What?" Dad says, seriously. His face goes from defeated to concerned. "Why didn't you say anything?"

Is he kidding? "Well, I would have but I think you and Nancy are too busy fighting to listen."

"We're never too busy for you, Sam. You can tell us anything."

If only that were true in reverse. How do you trust someone who doesn't trust you? Even if it's your parents?

Dad takes my silence as an answer. "I mean it, Sam, no matter what happens, Nancy and I are always going to be here for you and your sister."

Was he kidding me with this? Good mood gone, I'm angry again. Always here for me? He can't even tell me the truth.

"There for me? Like you were there when I found out about Travel?" I ask.

"Of course," Dad says hesitantly, surprised at my tone. "Even though I wasn't home, we celebrated."

"And when were you planning to tell me I can't join the team because we're moving?"

Dad's mouth hangs open. He looks down. His shoes have suddenly become very interesting to him. He picks at them while I wait. Finally he looks up at me, though he doesn't look right into my eyes.

"How long have you known?" he asks.

That's it? No apology or anything? "For a while. Tasha saw the For Sale sign."

Dad nods but doesn't say anything more so I continue. "At first I thought it was wrong. I heard Nancy say something about a mistake about the house. But I saw my room online, talked to Mom, and heard you and Nancy talking about you losing your job."

Dad looks up surprised. "Me doing what?"

"Come on, Dad, are you really not going to tell me, even now? I'm not a baby, you know. I'm going into eighth grade. I'm practically in high school. We're going to live with your parents, I guess. And it's okay. I already spoke to someone on the team out there and they'll let me try out. But you could have told me."

Dad is silent. Rain falls in a constant stream on the roof. Thankfully nothing seems to be getting through.

"I didn't know what to say," Dad says at last.

"How 'bout the truth? I don't even understand why we need to move, Dad. You only lost your job this week. I've had plenty of friends with parents who lost their jobs. They still live in Stamford."

"It's complicated," Dad says. "But I haven't lost my job."

He hasn't? Then why are we moving? "Now I really don't understand. You've been worried about money and I heard Nancy say something about a new job."

"I'm not sure what you mean about money. I never like wasting it though, which is why I didn't want to pay twice. I still have my job, but in many ways it will be new. The company is moving some of its people. I thought I'd be fine, but they need me to go too."

That's a relief. "So we don't have to live with your parents?"

Dad shakes his head no. "But you have it wrong, Sam. We really are going to Wyoming just to visit. My new job's in Portland, Oregon."

Portland, Oregon? I had finally gotten used to the idea of moving to Wyoming, had things all worked out with baseball, and now he throws me this curve? I don't even know what to say. "I have to go get ready for bed," I tell him.

"We should probably bring Nancy and Deborah their toothbrushes too," Dad says. "I don't think they want to walk back to the bathrooms tonight."

Whatever, I think in my head. I gather up my toiletries, grab an umbrella, and head out into the rain. It's still coming down hard enough I feel like I'm all by myself instead of walking next to Dad. I can't believe this. If he'd been honest with me I wouldn't have wasted time looking in the wrong place. And Oregon? That's on the complete opposite side of the country. Not that Wyoming isn't, but at least my grandparents are there. We know no one in Oregon.

We almost pass Nancy and Deborah in the rain. Dad stops them and hands them their things. I follow them to the bathroom. Nancy is so wrapped up in her own anger she doesn't even ask me what's wrong.

We finish and head back to the tent. As soon as we get back I take off my socks, which are now soaking wet, and climb into my sleeping bag, wishing this whole night had been one bad dream.

When I wake up it takes a minute or two to get used to the dark tent. Streams of light slip around the sides in places the tarp didn't cover. I pull on some sweat pants and head outside.

A layer of mist hangs on everything and climbs about halfway up the side of the hills. The morning sun gives everything a strange glow. The air feels new, as if the rain cleaned it somehow. In the distance horses are neighing and moving with thumps and clops.

Anxious to explore this strange world, I text a note to Nancy, walk over to Mike's tent, and listen for sounds.

"You up?" I text him. I count to twenty, staring at the phone as if I could wake him with my thoughts. No response. Oh well.

As I walk down the gravel road, quiet voices whisper secret words inside the tents, adding to the make-believe feeling of the morning. I can almost imagine this is just a normal vacation and not the end of life as I know it.

After using the bathroom, I check my phone, missing Tasha. The horses are in their pen, calm and quiet, eating grass. Their tails move like fans behind them and they don't seem so menacing now. Climbing up on the fence, I dangle my legs over. My mind turns to my conversation with Dad. Oregon.

A cold, wet nuzzle on my hand wakes me up.

The grey horse stands in front of me, its nose resting against my palm. The horse's eyes look deep into mine. *"Hi, Misty,"* I whisper

"Looks like you made a new friend."

My heart jumps in surprise and I almost fall off the fence. Mike stands next to me. I'd been so involved with the horse, I hadn't heard him approach.

"Sorry," he says. "I got your text. I didn't mean to startle you."

"You didn't," I say.

He looks at me.

"Okay, you did, but it's fine. I was just saying hi to Deborah's horse."

"The one who tried to run her over?"

Laughing I say, "Yeah, that too. But he's also been in a story I've been telling her. In the story she is the Princess of horses and her best friend is a grey horse just like this one. I called it Misty."

"Is that why she thought she could stop them yesterday? A story?"

I nod.

"Four-year-olds."

"I know, right? But maybe that's easier, being four I mean. It's definitely not so easy being thirteen."

"You spoke to your dad, didn't you?" Mike says.

"How can you tell?"

"I can always tell when something's going on with you. I just don't always know what to do or say to help. So what'd he say?"

"He didn't lose his job."

"That's great!"

My raised hand tells him to stop. "He is being transferred. To Oregon."

"Oregon? What happened to Wyoming? We researched Wyoming."

I take a deep breath in and out. Mike places his hands on my shoulders and holds on tight. "Look, whether it's Wyoming or Oregon doesn't matter. What matters is we find a way to make this better."

He puts his arm around my shoulder, then pulls me closer so my body rests against him. I don't tell him about the email. There's no point. But for right now, this moment, with Mike holding me, I almost feel like things will be okay.

"Come on," Deborah calls. "Daddy says we're going to see some giants and that they're not at all scary."

"Giants?" I ask Mike. He shrugs and helps me off the fence. We walk back to the car, only dropping hands as we get in view of the tents. "I wish I could ride with you," I tell him.

"I'm sure it would be okay with my parents."

"Let's go!" Deborah says.

THE PERFECT TRIP

Tilting my head toward Deborah, I shrug and head to my car. Mike nods in understanding. Nancy sits up front looking forward, not giving my dad a moment of her time. We travel a little ways until we come to a place where the road goes under a mountain. As soon as we go through the tunnel, Deborah's giants come into view. Four of them—well, their heads anyway.

"Daddy, there are men in the mountain!" Deborah yells.

"Welcome to Mount Rushmore," Dad says.

We pull into the visitor's parking lot and walk over to the viewing area. Mike and his family go inside to use the bathroom. Dad puts money into a telescope and we each take turns looking at the giant heads.

"Who are they?" Deborah asks.

This one I know. "Those are our most famous presidents: Washington, Lincoln, Jefferson, and Roosevelt. But Franklin or Teddy?" I ask Dad.

"Franklin, I think. Maybe Teddy, you know I'm not sure. Let me look."

He looks through the telescope and says, "Franklin. Definitely."

Nancy moves him aside and looks. "You are wrong, Jeff. That's Teddy."

"I guess we'll have to wait and see," Dad says.

"I guess we will," she snaps back.

We go into the Visitor's Center. Dad reads through the information.

"Nancy's right! It's Teddy."

"Don't sound so shocked. You're not the only one who knows a thing or two about history," Nancy says.

Their voices are getting slightly louder. Jim and Amy have walked over to another side of the exhibit. Mike gives me a look, but stays by his parents.

"Oh really, Nancy," Dad says playfully. "Then tell me when Teddy Roosevelt was president."

Quickly, I scan the information to find the dates before she answers.

Nancy says, "1901 – 1909."

She's right. Dad knows it too. But instead he says, "Lucky guess."

"Oh really, is that so? And I am sure the law degree I have was just lucky too? My bar exam score? Luck?"

"Nancy, calm down," Dad says.

"I am tired of being calm, Jeff. And I'm tired of you thinking you're always right. Sometimes it's okay to listen to the ideas of others."

Dad puts up his hands in defeat. Nancy shakes her head and walks in the direction of Mike's parents. What is this all about?

"Let's go outside," Dad says. We walk around a bit more to see Mount Rushmore from different angles. Unfortunately it is really far away and we're not allowed to get closer.

When we get back into the car, Nancy doesn't say anything. The car is as silent as the mountain of rock we just viewed.

Back at the campground they are set up for the cookout. "Deborah and I are going to ride in the wagon," Nancy says.

"But I want to ride a horse," Deborah whines.

"See the way the horses are pulling the wagon, and how there's a driver up front. That's because it's really a carriage," I tell her.

She looks at it, then at me. She tilts her head in a way that says she doesn't believe me, but then she shrugs her shoulders and puts on her crown. As they walk away, she looks longingly at the horses, but she goes anyway.

"What's going on with you and Nancy?" I ask Dad. He's already told me everything, he might as well share this too.

"Nothing," he says.

Seriously?

"So, have you picked a horse?" a man asks from behind me.

The grey horse comes to mind right away. "Yes," I say, "I would like to ride that one." I point to Misty.

"Oh, you don't want to ride ol' Stormy," the man says. "That one has a real temper."

Stormy, not Misty, looks at me with his deep brown eyes. He doesn't look mean. I can't believe the gentle creature that nudged my hand is really a wild beast.

"I really would like to ride him if that's okay."

"Do you have riding experience?" the man asks.

I've been horseback riding a couple of times, but nothing too significant. However, the man doesn't know that.

"Yeah," I lie. "I've been on horses loads of times."

The man looks at my dad. Dad's eyes are on Nancy so he nods in approval even though he has no idea what the man's asking. He gets on a horse and heads up behind them, leaving me alone. Jim and Amy follow him after Amy stops by Mike. She whispers something to him, and takes off.

"Okay," the man says, taking my dad's leave as approval. "You be sure to hold on tight."

He leads me over to Stormy and helps me get on. Stormy looks up at me as if to welcome me on board. Deborah will be so excited to see me riding her horse.

Mike finds a brown spotted horse. He climbs on and pulls alongside me. "Hey, you got Misty," he says.

"I did, though his real name is Stormy. Who's this?" I ask, pointing to his horse.

"This is Al."

Al looks up at his name. We both laugh.

"So what did your mom want?" I ask him.

"The usual be careful stuff. She also told me to keep an eye on you and make sure you were safe."

Mike's horse takes a step closer and I can feel Stormy tense up. I pat him on the neck and whisper, "This is how you help me, by scaring my horse? It's okay, Stormy, Al's not going to bother you."

"Oops," Mike says. He moves Al a little further away.

Other people arrive and get on horses or in the wagon. Dad trots close to the wagon, trying to get Nancy's attention. She ignores him.

Finally it's time to go. We trot along single file, up a path through the hills. I look up ahead at Nancy and

THE PERFECT TRIP

Deborah in the wagon. Deborah sits up very tall, a true princess sitting in a horse drawn carriage. Dad, Jim, and Amy are next in line. Mike's closer to me, but a couple of other riders have moved in between us.

After a little while the woods grow thick around us. We continue up the hill. So far no problems from Stormy. I don't know what the man is talking about.

We pass a stream. Suddenly Stormy roams off the path and into the water.

"Hey," I say, pulling back on the reigns. "Stormy, you're going the wrong way."

Stormy ignores me and continues heading for the water. He bends down and takes a drink.

A man from the ranch pulls up beside us. "Stormy," he says, "you know this is not the way." He leans over to grab the reins.

Stormy arches his neck and snorts. He lifts his back leg and kicks at the man's horse. "Whoa, boy," the man says. Stormy snorts and I can feel him lifting again.

I grip the reigns as hard as I can. But as he rears up to kick again, I lose my balance. I try to stay on, but I can feel my body slipping.

All at once I'm wet and cold and my hand hurts. I'm sitting in the stream, way too close to this crazy horse. Stormy continues to kick, barely missing my head. I scramble through the water to get away. How could they let me take this horse?

"Sam, what happened?" a voice says. I look up and see a brown and white horse.

"Mike!" I sigh. He slides off his horse and helps me out of the stream.

"Are you okay?" he asks.

"Uh huh," I say. My arms shake. I take in a good breath and examine myself. I'm wet from the bottom down and my right hand hurts, but nothing seems too serious. I've experienced worse during ball games. I turn my hand over and see a small gash in my palm. It's bleeding slightly, but not gushing.

"I don't think anything's broken," I say a bit more confidently. "But I'm wet and dirty and I could use a Band-Aid." Plus I'm a little nervous about what

Nancy will say when she sees me. Will this be another reason for her to be mad at Dad?

"Do you want to forget this and go back?" Mike asks.

"I want to stay. Besides, I insisted on the horse."

"Why'd you do that?" Mike asks.

"For a few minutes there I thought I was four."

Mike laughs.

The ranch guys surround Stormy and seem to have completely forgotten about me. Fortunately Mike is here otherwise I'd be sitting bleeding in a stream. The two of us walk the rest of the way to the cookout with Al walking next to us. As soon as Deborah sees us she runs over gushing with excitement.

"Sammy, I *was* in a real carriage! They pulled me just like a princess! I even saw the horse poop!"

Nancy wasn't as excited to see us. "What happened?" she asks, rushing over. "Why are you walking and why don't you have a horse?"

"I'm fine, Nancy, don't worry."

She still looks worried. Her eyes are pinched together in a frown. I hide my hand from her.

"We should go check out the barbecue," I tell Mike. "Come on, Deb." We give Al to a ranch hand and I drag them away before she can examine me further.

The man from the corral finds me and asks to see my hand.

He looks me over, up and down. "So, I see I was right about Stormy," he says. "I think I have something that can help with that."

He turns around and grabs a first aid kit. He takes out some peroxide and a bandage.

"This might hurt a bit," he says as he pours the peroxide on my hand. It stings. I wince but keep a smile on my face in case Nancy's watching.

Once the bandage is on I feel much better. Mike and I grab some burgers and Deborah takes us over to where everyone is sitting.

For the next hour we sing campfire songs, eat more hot dogs and hamburgers, and enjoy sitting in the fresh night air. I almost forget Nancy and Dad's fight and the fact we're moving to Oregon, not Wyoming. Almost.

THE PERFECT TRIP

When it's time to go the man from the corral says, "Now there is one more thing we have to show you, especially you city folk."

One of the other horse hands takes a bucket of sand and throws it on the fire. Smoke billows around us and we can't see anything. Just like that, we're alone under the night sky.

There are more stars then I've ever seen. Tiny gold lights flashing in a perfect black background. I feel like I'm sitting in a Planetarium. It's almost too perfect to be real.

No one says anything. Then one of the leaders whispers, "Before the white men came to this land it was home to my people, the Indian. We believe that each of our great warriors and leaders found a place in the sky when they left this earth."

His words fill me with chills. I'm not even disappointed riding in the wagon back to camp because it means I can keep looking at the sky and forget my problems.

20

By the time we get back to the tent it's too late to talk. Dad sleeps next to me again so he's definitely not done fighting with Nancy. We wake up early, take down the tents, and say goodbye to South Dakota.

As we pull out, I see Stormy standing by the fence. "You know what, Sammy?" Deborah says. "That's not Misty."

"I know, Deb. His name is Stormy."

She nods. "I know who *he* is. He's Misty's evil twin brother. He tricked Princess Samantha into riding him so he could hurt her. But Prince Michael was there to save the day."

My mouth turns from a frown to a grin. "That's a great story, Deb. Really great."

"I know! It's like one you tell," Deb says. "And do you see how I got Mike in it?"

I did. "I'm sure he'll love that."

She smiles and hums to herself as she looks out the window. I expect Nancy to be smiling at us too, but she's busy typing on her phone. I don't think she's heard Deborah at all.

Dad glances over and shakes his head. He looks at us in the rearview mirror. "Well, guys, today we are going back in time to the Old West."

"What do you mean, Daddy? Like cowboys and stuff?" Deborah asked.

"Exactly like cowboys and stuff. But it is going to take a while to get there so hunker down," Dad said.

"Huh?"

"He is just trying to talk cowboy. He means get comfortable," Nancy says flatly.

"Okay," Deborah answers. She pulls out all of the princesses from her bag and lines them up in the pocket on the back of Nancy's seat so their arms and heads peek out. "Today I am going to tell you the story of Princess Deborah," she says to them.

Now this is a change. Off story duty, I take out my music, close my eyes, and wish on the stars we saw last night that there won't be any opportunities to ride horses in this Old West.

We stop to eat burritos at a little place by the side of the road. "How are you doing?" Mike asks. He takes my hand and looks it over as if he can see through the Band-Aid.

"I'm okay, but I still don't know what's going on with Dad and Nancy. They aren't even talking."

"Really?" Mike says. With all the baseball stuff, I hadn't even told him about that until now. "You've never mentioned the fighting before."

"I've never seen them fight before. She's been on her phone since we left the campground." I think about this for a few minutes. "Do you think she could be trying to leave him? Maybe she's looking for flights back home."

Mike shakes his head. "That's crazy. Besides, aren't they selling your house? Even if she wanted to leave, she has nowhere to go."

I drop my head, wishing he hadn't reminded me of that. But Nancy's parents live in Brooklyn. Couldn't she stay with them?

"I think you're letting your story telling go to your head," Mike says. "Even if Nancy and your dad are in a fight, that doesn't mean she'd leave him. Nothing happens that quickly, you know."

Except I don't know that at all. When my mom left my dad and me, it *was* that quick. I woke up one morning and she was standing at the door with her bags packed, telling me she'd see me soon.

"Nancy is not your mom," Mike says.

That's true, Nancy's not Mom, but that means if Nancy were to leave Dad, she wouldn't have any reason to see me. I finally have someone who loves me like a mother. I can't lose that again. And life without Deborah underfoot is unthinkable.

Mike gives me a hug and I get back into the car. Deborah falls asleep. At about four o'clock we pull into Old Trail Town and the late 1800s.

It's exactly what my dad promised, a town right out of Old West movies, or at least what the Old West looked like in *Blazing Saddles*, since that's the only Old West movie I've seen. There's a bunch of false front buildings surrounded by wagons and horses, all back dropped against dirt roads and mountains. We park and meet Mike and his parents in front of the general store.

"Look, dress up!" Deborah yells. She drags Mike and me over to a storefront where there's a woman taking pictures. She has a bunch of dress up clothes behind her.

"I want to dress up like an Old West person!" Deborah begs.

"I don't know, honey," Nancy says. I can tell she's not in the mood for anything fun.

"Oh please, Mommy? Please, please, please!" Deborah whines.

"Please?" Dad says to Nancy. She glares at him. "Oh come on, Nancy, how often do we get to play Old West Dress Up?" He goes inside and tries on a black vest and cowboy hat. Jim follows and takes a similar vest and hat. Mike shrugs and does the same.

Deborah doesn't have to be asked twice. She runs in and grabs the frilliest dress that might fit and is in it in seconds. Nancy and Amy go through the clothes a bit slower, carefully picking things out that don't expose too much. They choose two frilly umbrellas as well.

If everyone else is doing it, I might as well. I pick the least puffy dress I can find. Pulling it on and looking in the mirror, I feel like it's still missing something. I pull a purple hat off a shelf. The bend in the hat slightly covers my face.

We take our pose in front of some faded wallpaper. "Now remember not to smile," the woman says.

"Not to smile?" Deborah asks.

"Yes, the people of the Old West never smiled in pictures."

Well, at least that works for us. She takes a bunch of shots and then we're finished. Everyone pulls off the clothes and walks outside. Everyone except Deborah.

"Deborah, take off your costume please," orders Nancy.

"No!" Deborah says.

We all stop what we're doing and look at her.

"Deb, listen to your mother and take the costume off. Other people want to get their pictures taken," Dad says.

I look around and see no one in sight but decide not to mention it. Deborah's face is tight and determined. This is going to take a while.

"It's not fair," she wails. "I don't have my wings or my crown. I want to wear this dress. I want to wear it NOW!"

Nancy's face grows slightly red. She tilts her head and opens her mouth to let Deborah have it. In her current mood, this is going to be a doozy. But the camerawoman breaks in before she can start.

"You know, it's a slow day. If she wants to wear the dress as you explore the town, it's okay with me. Frankly, you all can get dressed up. I'm sure our visitors will love it."

Nancy gives her a sharp look but Dad answers first. "That would be great, thanks."

Nancy glares at him, but Deborah pulls at her arm. "Come on, Mommy! Wear the dress! Please."

Nancy's mouth softens and she slowly forces herself to smile at Deborah. "Okay, sweetie, for you." She motions to Amy and the two of them go back into the changing room. I wait until they're done, not sure I want to hear Nancy talking about my dad if that's what she's doing.

When I come back out in my dress, the dads and Mike have already changed into their gear. This time my dad added bullet holders crossed over his chest, two revolvers, and things that go over the pants. I'm not sure what any of them are called, but they look great or completely silly depending on your attitude. For Deborah, I'm determined to get into this, though I'm glad the rules say I don't have to smile.

But Deborah's all smiles as she walks through the town with her Old West family. Visitors smile at us. They probably think we work here. Tourists even stop to take our pictures and I hide my face. No way I'm going viral. I'll never live it down at home...or at least I wouldn't if we were going back home. The reality of moving hasn't set in.

Deborah loves the attention. She strikes a different pose for every picture, making sure not to smile, of course. After a few minutes my dad gets into it too. Jeff and Amy join him.

"Come on," Mike says to me. "What do you have to lose?"

"My dignity?" I respond.

"Forget that. Why not have a little fun?"

I shrug, but let him lead me over to the group. Nancy has stayed by Deborah's side and is participating too. We must look completely ridiculous but everyone loves it. A guy even hands my dad a tip. "Maybe we should just live here," Dad whispers to Nancy. She doesn't laugh.

Right before closing time we go back to the photo place and return the clothes. This time Deborah doesn't have a fit.

We get into the car and drive away. Dad has a silly grin on his face, the one he gets before he tells us we're going to see something cool, but recognizing Nancy's still in a mood, he doesn't say anything. We drive into the town of Cody, Wyoming. Cody might not have been made up as old as the place we visited that morning, but it definitely has an old-time feel. We pass two men standing on the street corner and they are dressed up for real in Old West clothes.

"What's going on?" I ask Dad.

"You'll see," Dad says.

We park and walk with Mike's family to an open street. Jim tells us to take a seat on the ground. Mike sits next to me and gives me a questioning look. "The way things are going, I wouldn't be surprised it we are going back in time," I tell him.

THE PERFECT TRIP

After a few minutes of waiting, the two dressed up men walk out into the street from opposite sides. "Are they having a gun fight?" I whisper to Mike.

"I think so," he whispers back. "Cool."

Deborah takes my hand. "What are they doing, Sammy?"

Uh, oh. I think fast. "Playing pretend like we did this morning."

"Ohhh," she says.

The men say a few fighting words, turn, and shoot each other. One guy goes down in a real dramatic way, taking ten minutes to die. "Die already!" Deborah calls to him. "He's not a good actor," she says to me. I can't help but laugh.

After they're finished we go into one of those real "old fashion" ice cream shops where all the flavors are homemade. Even Nancy is smiling as she eats her sundae. But as soon as we're back in the car her bad mood returns. Maybe baseball isn't as important as finding a way for Dad and Nancy to work things out together.

Before we go to sleep Dad tells us we'll be in no rush tomorrow so everyone takes their time getting ready. Nancy and Amy take a walk with Deborah. Without Nancy there, Dad's mood brightens. "Let's play some Frisbee," he says. Jeff, Mike, and I get into position and we start to toss it around.

As soon as Amy and Nancy get back, Dad excuses himself and goes in the tent. Whatever is going on with them is getting worse. Nancy follows him in and Deborah walks behind her. That won't be good.

"Do you want play Frisbee, Deb?" I call to her.

She bounces over and away from the tent. "I want to play but I don't want to play Frisbee," she says. Great, more baby or princess. But if it will keep her busy, I'll do it. Maybe she can get Mike to wear wings or a crown.

"Okay, Deb," I say. "What do you want to play?"

"Gunfight!" she squeals. She holds up her fingers and says, "Boom, boom."

Mike and I look at each other and smile. We each draw out our fingers. "Bang!" I yell.

"Bang! Bang!" Mike says.

"Not like that," Deborah says.

"Then how do you want to do it?" I ask.

"You go over there and I stay here. We count to three and turn around and shoot, okay, Sam?"

So I'm Sam now. "Okay, Deb," I say. I begin walking away.

"Wait!" she yells.

"What?" I ask.

"Call me Dave."

Mike laughs but I don't think it's so funny. "Deb, there's no reason why you can't be a girl gunfighter."

"Right," Mike says.

"Now are we ready?" I ask.

"Yes," she says. I turn around and start walking.

"WAIT!" she screams again.

Mike's cracking up. "What is it now?" I ask.

Before I can stop her, she runs inside the tent. I hold my breath, but less than a second later she comes right back out holding her princess crown and wings. "Now I'm ready," she says. "I'm a gun fighting princess."

We take turns "killing each other." After the first dramatic deaths, Mike wants in too. Deborah's favorite is the quick fall. I like to play it up a bit more, coming back to life at least three or four times before finally kicking the bucket. Jim and Amy sit down to watch. We must look like such kids, which is why it is completely embarrassing when a man pulls up in a car. "Is Mrs. Barrette here?"

"I can get her," Amy says. She goes into the tent and Nancy comes out behind her. Dad comes out after them.

"Mrs. Barrette, you have a call in the main office. It sounds important," the man says. His voice is gruff, which makes the words sound as serious as their message.

"Thank you," Nancy says to the man. She turns to Amy, "Why don't you guys start lunch?"

"You don't think it's anything serious, do you?" Amy asks.

"I'm sure everything is fine," Nancy says. I stare at her for any sign of what's going on. A slight smile forms at the curve of her mouth.

Nancy gets into the man's car. I have a sudden, weird feeling I'm not going to see her again, but there's no way she'd leave Deborah behind.

We get lunch ready and eat, mostly, in silence. Even Deborah is bothered by Nancy's sudden disappearance. She sits right next to Dad and doesn't talk much either.

Nancy comes back about forty-five minutes later.

"Everything all right?" Amy asks as soon as we see her.

"Yes, it should be fine," Nancy says. She doesn't give us any more information but her mood is definitely lighter as she helps clean up and take down the tent. For some reason, though, Dad's mood has darkened.

"Come on, Sam, let's see if we can get the tent down the fastest ever," Dad says. "We're running late."

That's a knock on Nancy but she just shakes her head and smiles wider. Dad pulls apart pieces of the campsite, rolling and folding sleeping bags and throwing them into the car, pulling out stakes and packing things up. I help, with little thought on the matter at hand. Instead my focus is on Dad, stomping around us as if he's just heard the worst news in the world. What could it possibly mean?

My dad tells us the road he's chosen from Cody to Jackson Hole is very windy and will take us over the Rocky Mountains.

"I'm scared, Sammy," Deborah says when we get in the car. "I don't like going up mountains."

I don't tell her she's never experienced mountains like the ones we're about to see. Nothing on the East Coast is close to as high.

"So what was the call about?" I ask Nancy.

"I can't really say right now," she says, looking at Deborah. "But I have a possible way to fix our current situation."

"What sit-woo-ation, Mommy?" Deborah asks.

"Nothing to worry about, Deborah. There's been a. . .possibility that Sam wouldn't be able to play baseball this year. But I think I've solved that problem."

This makes me sit up straighter. What does she mean? Did she find a way for me to try out in Oregon? Or is she trying to talk about the move without saying anything to Deborah?

"I think we should talk about this later," Dad says.

"But why, Daddy?" Deborah says. "Don't you want Sammy to play baseball?"

Dad doesn't say anything. Deborah looks at me for some information, but I just shrug. I have no idea what's going on. She takes out her princesses and starts playing. I run though all the possibilities but can't think of any reason why Dad wouldn't be happy. I don't understand what's going on and why he still won't tell me.

For the first time all trip, our car is in front instead of Mike's. Our destination today is my grandparent's house. But first we have to cross the mountains. I look out the window and watch as they loom nearer. Looking up I can see snow circling their tops like whipped cream on an ice cream sundae. It's pretty impressive, but now it seems unimportant.

We travel further up the road and pull into an overlook. Mike's car follows us. Without giving the rest of us a chance to catch up, Dad gets out of the car and walks right over to the edge. I think he did it because he knows it makes Nancy crazy. The rest of us stand closer to the car and look out. It's one of the most beautiful sights on the trip. I bet we can see all the way back to South Dakota.

Mike comes over and takes my hand. "What's going on?" he asks.

"Nancy says she has a way for me to play baseball but Dad doesn't seem happy about it. I didn't even realize he'd told her that I knew."

"That's great though, Sam. I'm sure it'll work out if Nancy says she's found a way."

I hope so. I hate that now they seem to be fighting about me.

We get back into the car and continue winding our way over the mountains. Deborah falls asleep. I try to wake her up to see the amazing views but she's done. I put my earphones on but turn off the sound when Dad starts talking to Nancy.

"I'm not going to let you take it," he says.

"Not going to *let* me? Who do you think you are?"

"Your husband who loves you and knows this is not what you want."

"Who says?"

"You have. I've heard you tell your friends how much you love being home with Deborah."

I lean in a bit closer, wishing I could take out my earphones without them noticing.

"I *do* love that Deborah has a parent at home with her, but that wouldn't change. You're just being selfish and pigheaded. And what about Sam? She's worked so hard to get on the team. You really want to throw that away?"

There they go, fighting about me again.

"She'll make a new team," Dad says.

"When, next year? That's not fair."

"Nancy, be reasonable."

"You're the one not being reasonable. And I'm done talking about this. As soon as we get to your parents, I'm leaving. You're going to have to accept it."

Leaving? My eyes open wide and I close them quickly before they notice. I was right. Nancy *is* leaving Dad. How could this have happened?

I can't let Nancy leave Dad because of me. If it will keep Dad and Nancy together, I'll never play baseball again.

Before I get a chance to talk to them, we pull into my grandparent's driveway. "Ooo, big!" Deborah says. My grandparent's house is pretty spectacular. I've seen pictures, but it looks even more impressive in person.

The house is made of logs but is like no log cabin I've ever seen. It's very long and has two separate doorways, one that has a high triangular arched entrance. Through the other doorway I can see an outdoor stone fireplace. If I wasn't so upset about Nancy I'd be very excited to explore this place further. Snow-topped mountains rise in the distance over a lake.

But before I take in anything else my eyes fall on the black car outside the house.

"Are you leaving right now?" I ask Nancy.

She looks at me for a minute, probably trying to figure out what I know. Deborah sits up in her booster seat. "Mommy, you're leaving?"

"Yes, Deborah, but don't worry. Your grandparents will be here to help Dad out, and Mike's family too."

"But I want you," Deborah says. "Who will put me to sleep?" Her bottom lip is quivering.

"I'll be back in a few days and Sam can put you to bed until I get back," Nancy says.

"It's not the same," Deborah says.

Nancy releases her from her booster seat and Deborah hops out and marches past her into the arms of my waiting grandparents. They've gotten older since we saw them last and both seem to have shrunk a bit. If you look closely, past the grey hair and wrinkles, you can see how much my grandpa looks like my dad. My grandma wears an apron and has her hair in curls. She opens her arms and Deborah climbs in.

"What's this about?" Granny asks Nancy.

"Sorry, Betsy. Deborah just found out I'm leaving."

Granny nods. "Don't worry, Debbie. Mom will be back before you know it. We have lots of fun things to do out here."

THE PERFECT TRIP

Nancy says goodbye to Amy and Jim, gives Deborah a hug, and moves to say goodbye to me. "Take care of your sister, okay, Sam?" she says.

"Don't go, Nancy," I whisper to her. "Please."

She kisses me on the head. "Everything will be fine. You'll see."

We watch her limo pull away. There's a pain deep in my chest, one I haven't felt in years. The pain of losing a mom.

Mike comes over and takes my hand. He doesn't ask me if I'm okay. He knows I'm not.

"Come inside, you two," my grandpa calls from the steps.

Mike squeezes my hand and the two of us walk inside. We enter a large room with a high ceiling. Wood logs crisscross above our heads. To our left is an enormous island, which is part of an even bigger kitchen. But the most amazing thing is the view out the windows. Above the tree line stand more snow-covered mountains. Below them we can see a lake of pure blue.

"It's too bad you aren't moving here," Mike whispers in my ear. I punch his shoulder.

Mike and I walk around the rest of the house. There's five bedrooms, one for my grandparents, one for Deborah and me, one for Mike's parents, one for Mike, and one for my dad. Dad's room looks so empty without Nancy's big suitcase. She's brought it home with her. Do they really think I wouldn't notice that?

I leave Mike in his room. Dad's busy bringing in things from the car. He seems to be completely unaffected by Nancy's sudden departure. "Aren't you upset?" I ask.

"It's no big deal, Sam," Dad says. "Nancy and I don't see eye to eye on this, but I can't stop her from leaving."

What? He's not even going to try?

"This is what happened with Mom, isn't it? She left and you did absolutely nothing."

"That's not true and not the same. I begged your mom to stay. But sometimes you have to know when you've lost."

"I don't understand you. Anytime someone stands in my way you tell me to fight. How can you just give up?"

Dad looks at me, his head back like I've wounded him somehow. "This isn't the same thing, Sam."

I shake my head. "You were supposed to be the one I could count on."

He reaches for my arm. "Of course you can count on me. How many times do I need to say it?"

I shake my head. "It's not enough to say it. You have to live it." I run away from him and out the back door. I'm so tired of his lies and lack of action. For the first time in years I have someone I think of as a mom and he is willing to let her go just like that. It's not fair. None of this is fair!

I sit on the porch not sure whether to scream or cry. A shadow hangs over my head. I look up into Deborah's eyes.

"Sammy, I want to see the lake," she says.

"So?" I ask, knowing exactly what she's talking about but deciding to be difficult.

"Please, Sammy, please take me exploring! We can even play more baseball," Deborah begs. She pulls out my bat and ball from behind her.

I'm about to say no, but why not? I can see a rowboat by the dock. I've paddled one before. Across the lake is the perfect place to be. As far from Dad as possible. I want Mike to come too, but there's no way I'm going back into that house.

"Come on, Deb," I say. "Let's go boating."

23

My body trembles as I look across the never-ending lake. I can scarcely believe about an hour ago these waters represented a needed escape. What do they mean now?

"Sammy, I want to go home," Deborah wails.

"I'm trying, Deb, I'm trying." I take in a deep breath and imagine myself on the mound facing down a pitcher. I breathe in and out. Using that focus, I look around. The shore must be around here someplace. I know I paddled straight but even from my calm place, nothing seems familiar.

How could this have happened? Everything seemed to be going well. We found some life jackets and I untied the boat. Deborah got in and I pushed us off. The sound of the water in my ears drowned out the yelling and screaming in my head. I was so mad. Angry at Dad for letting this happen. Angry at Nancy for not trying harder. Deborah pulled me out of my head by saying, "Sammy, aren't we still really far away?" That's when I looked up.

The sky had turned to shades of pink and Deborah was right, the opposite shore was still far away. Even if I was able to get there before dark, we wouldn't be able to come back.

"Let's turn around," I told her. She nodded. But when I turned the boat I realized that where the house should be, the only thing I could see was trees. I've been paddling forward since, but still nothing.

"Sammy, I'm cold. I want to go home!" Deborah cries again. She cowers on her seat, looking at me as if I can work a miracle. But I'm not Princess Samantha and there's no Misty to save us. I wish there was.

I hold one oar tightly under my arm and pull out my phone again. Something has to be working. Text? GPS? But when I've opened Maps, it's just a blank screen searching. I feel the same way.

I look back at the mountains. Their snow-topped peaks laugh at me. Snow in July. Ridiculous.

"Sammy, I want to go home, NOW!"

"Me too, Deb, me too," I cry with her.

THE PERFECT TRIP

Suddenly I hear voices. At first they're quiet whispers in the distance. I'm not even completely sure they're human. The voices expand into our names, "Sam! Deborah!" Over and over again.

"Deb, they've found us!" I cry. She lifts her head up to look. "Over here!" I yell as loud as I can. "We're over here."

I bring the paddles into the rowboat and take off my life jacket. I place it on the edge of my bat and hold it up high like a flag. Not too far away are three canoes. They spot the bright orange jacket and head for us. Leading the charge in the head canoe is Nancy.

"Nancy, over here!" I scream. "Deborah, do you see? It's Nancy and Dad."

"Mommy!" Deborah says.

Moments later, they're finally here: Nancy, Dad, Mike, Jim, Amy, and my grandparents. They surround the boat and quickly have us reorganized. Dad takes over my paddles and I move to where Deborah was sitting. She, in turn, is taken into the boat with Nancy.

Dad unties my life vest from my bat and tells me to wear it. Once I'm settled in, Mike puts a blanket around my shoulders. "I was so scared," he says.

"Why didn't you tell me you were going?" I'm too cold to answer.

We head back to shore. The blanket cuddles me in warmth so comforting my eyes start to tear. I notice there's a lot of other teary-eyed people as well.

"I'm sorry," I say to my dad.

"We'll talk more about it later. Right now we're just glad you and Deborah are safe."

As we get closer I realize my mistake. The dock lies around a small bend in the lake. If I'd kept going straight I would have seen it. It had been there the whole time.

When we finally arrive at the dock, an ambulance sits in the parking lot. Grandpa gets out and lets them know we're okay.

Dad carries Deborah into the house and I follow behind, next to Nancy. "You came back," I say to her.

"I did. As soon as your dad told me you disappeared I had the limo turn around. I'll take the red eye instead."

Wait, she's still leaving?

I stop her by holding her arm. "No, Nancy, you can't leave us. We need you too much. I don't have to play baseball. It's not important."

"What are you talking about, Sam?"

"I heard you and Dad talking. I know you're leaving him because of me."

Nancy bites her lip and motions me over to the benches by the outdoor fireplace. A small fire has been started and it feels so nice and cozy. "I'm not leaving you or your father, Sam. You're my family."

I don't understand. "Then why are you going home? And why's Dad so upset?"

"I have a job interview. If it works out, and I think it might, we won't have to leave Stamford."

Wait, what?

"But what about Dad and his job?"

"It's a bit complicated, but your dad will get something called severance, which basically means his company will pay for him to stay home for a while to look for a new job close by."

Everything she's saying matches the conversation I heard between her and Dad, about her not being able to stay home with Deborah and the fact that someone will be home with her. Nancy meant Dad would be home. I'd gotten things wrong again.

"Why couldn't the two of you just tell me the truth? I've been so upset thinking Dad is out of work, thinking we were moving, thinking you were leaving him. It's completely ruined everything!" Tears have started pouring out of my eyes. My nose is running. Nancy pulls me into a deep hug and waits while I let it all out.

"You're right," Nancy says. "We should have. But sometimes adults make mistakes too. We think we're protecting you when really we're making things worse. Your dad and I are both very, very sorry."

We sit in silence for a few minutes, watching the flames in the fireplace. "So we're not moving?" I ask.

"We don't know what we're doing yet. I still have to interview for the job and get it, and your dad still has to be okay with leaving his job and finding another one. But, Sam, I promise that when we figure it out you'll be the first to know. And whatever happens, we'll figure it out together."

"And Dad will do that too?"

"Why don't you ask him?"

Dad walks over with Deborah. He holds Nancy's hand for a moment, then she gets up and gives me a big hug before taking Deborah back inside.

"I'm sorry," Dad says. "Your mom told me I was making a mistake in not letting you know what was going on. For once she was right."

I think about that for a moment. "If Mom really wanted to help, she would have told you I knew. She didn't, did she?"

He shakes his head.

"About what I said, Dad, I'm sorry for thinking you'd let Nancy leave us. I do trust you and count on you. That's why this has been so hard."

He nods. "When it comes to what you said, you have nothing to be sorry for, Sam. You shouldn't have taken your sister out in the boat, but you know that already. The rest of the mistakes were mine."

"So what now?" I ask.

"Now I'm going to stop being stubborn and pig headed and see what happens with Nancy's job. If she gets it, things will be different."

"As long as we're all together, I think it will work out."

"Me too," Dad says. He gives me a big hug.

For the first time since Tasha saw the moving sign, I feel like everything is going to be okay.

24

Three days after the boat incident we sit in the same spot on the deck in front of the fire. Everyone is here together. Tomorrow Mike and his family are heading home. We're staying with my grandparents for a few more days and then we're flying back. Nancy's new job starts next week so they hired a service to transport the car.

Tasha got home yesterday.

"Well?" she asks the second she picks up the phone.

"We're not moving. It's definite this time."

"I'm so, so, so happy to hear it. I don't know what I'd do without you."

"What about Mia?"

"Mia is great, but she's like our parents' age now. And there's only one Sam."

I say goodbye and turn my attention back to the conversation in front of the fireplace.

"Sounds like it's been some trip," my grandmother says to everyone.

"Yes, and we're happy to be here with such good friends," Amy says. She gives Mike's arm a squeeze. "Hopefully this won't be the last time we go camping together."

Everyone looks at Nancy.

"What?" she says. We all look at her. "Okay, I have to admit that I didn't love sleeping in a tent or showering outside. But the campfires were great. I'm thinking we need to get a fire pit."

Dad puts his arm around her and kisses her on the cheek. "Only if we can also get a donkey."

"Jeff."

"The look on your face," Jim says. "I thought I was going to pee in my pants."

"Dad!" Mike says.

"And what about that rattlesnake sign?" Dad says.

"Yeah, Mommy, I thought you peed your pants when I showed it to you."

We all laugh.

"Deborah, let's not talk about peeing, okay?" Nancy says.

"But he said it," she points at Jim. He puts his hands up in defeat.

They continue telling stories about the trip. Looking back now, even the difficult parts were pretty incredible. Mike and I tell them about Deborah trying to stop the horses and about me falling into the stream. Nancy talks about the heart attack she felt like she was having watching us all at the edge of the canyon. Dad recalls the details of the corn murals at the Corn Palace.

We go on until the fire dies down. Mike pulls me up and we walk toward the lake. "So, you're not moving," he says.

I shake my head no.

"It'll definitely be weird with Nancy working and Dad at home, but I think it will all work out for them."

"What about for us?" Mike asks.

I look into his big blue eyes. I want to tell him things will work out for us too, but there's one thing holding me back.

"Mike, about Travel," I say.

He opens his mouth to cut in, but I'm not done. "What if I give up my spot so you can play?" I think about my dad and Nancy. "There are so many things more important than baseball."

"No, there isn't."

I open my mouth to protest, but he puts his finger to my lips. "I've known you a long time, Samantha Barrette. And I've spent this summer watching you fight for this. You aren't giving up baseball for me or anyone else. Not if I have any say anyway. Besides, there are always other Travel teams."

"What do you mean?"

"I mean, you aren't the only one who's been trying to find a way to play ball. As soon as we get home I'm trying out for another team. And if I make it…"

"You'll make it."

"When I make it, you'd better bring your best to the field because I have a pretty amazing arm."

"Yes, you do," I say, holding his shoulder. He leans in and kisses me! On the lips. It's light, and quick, and completely awkward. We both laugh as he pulls back.

But it turns out there *are* other things as great as baseball. After all we've been though, I've finally reached the sweet spot of this perfect trip.

ACKNOWLEDGMENTS

When I was eight years old my parents took me on a camping trip from New York to Wyoming and back. That trip was one of the best memories of my childhood and I've been trying to write about it ever since. The first attempt led me to my main character, Sam and the start of her story. I'm so thankful to finally find the right character to take camping.

Thank you to my critique group partners Joan Riordian, Nina Mansfield, Trevor Macomber, Norma Jean-Jacques, Mike Purfield, Dave Symonds, and Joyce Shor Johnson, and to my amazing beta readers Kimberly Sabitini, Paige and Kinsey Shockley, Chris Eboch, Sam Bond, Noah Tabossi Zugman, Adam Tulchinsky, and Lara Olmsted. Each new pair of eyes found something that made this story better.

Thank you to the students, staff, and parents of Riverside School for the constant encouragement.

Thank you to the team at Spellbound River Press. I'm so glad The Sweet Spot found its way to you.

A special thanks to my cover artist Lois Bradley. It's pretty incredible seeing your main character and her sister come alive in illustration

My acknowledgements would not be complete without thanking my husband, Gary, and my children Daniel and Annie. You give me the time to follow my dream. I wouldn't be a published author without your love and support.

ABOUT THE AUTHOR

Stacy Barnett Mozer is a third grade teacher and a mom. She started writing books when a class of students told her there was no way that a *real* author who wrote *real* books could possibly revise their work as much as she asked them to revise. She's been revising her own work ever since.

To learn more about Stacy, go to her website at www.stacymozer.com. You can follow her on twitter at @SMozer.

Stacy also blogs about girls in sports and sporty girl books. Visit sportygirlbooks.blogspot.com for book lists, interviews, and other sporty girl content.

Also by Stacy Barnett Mozer

The Sweet Spot

When thirteen-year-old Sam Barrette's baseball coach tells her that her attitude's holding her back, she wants to hit him in the head with a line drive. Why shouldn't she have an attitude? As the only girl playing in the 13U league, she's had to listen to boys and people in the stands screaming things like "Go play softball," all season, just because she's a girl. Her coach barely lets her play, even though she's one of the best hitters on the team.

All stakes now rest on Sam's performance at baseball training camp. But the moment she arrives, miscommunication sets the week up for potential disaster. Placed at the bottom with the weaker players, she will have to work her way up to A league, not just to show Coach that she can be the best team player possible, but to prove to herself that she can hold a bat with the All-Star boys.

Made in the USA
Middletown, DE
29 March 2017